Love and Lies

Also by Jane McBride Choate
in Large Print:

The Courtship of Katie McGuire
Love by the Book
Trust Me
Design to Deceive
Sweet Lies and Rainbow Skies

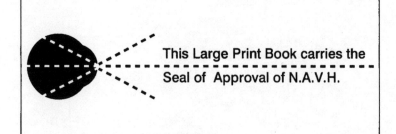

This Large Print Book carries the
Seal of Approval of N.A.V.H.

Love and Lies

Jane McBride Choate

Thorndike Press • Waterville, Maine

Published in 2003 by arrangement with
Jane McBride Choate.

Thorndike Press Large Print Candlelight Series.

The tree indicium is a trademark of Thorndike Press.

The text of this Large Print edition is unabridged.
Other aspects of the book may vary from the original edition.

Set in 16 pt. Plantin by Myrna S. Raven.

Printed in the United States on permanent paper.

Library of Congress Cataloging-in-Publication Data

Choate, Jane McBride.
    Love and lies / Jane McBride Choate.
      p. cm.
    ISBN 0-7862-4575-1 (lg. print : hc : alk. paper)
    1. Carpenters — Fiction. 2. Extortion — Fiction.
  3. Large type books. I. Title.
    PS3553.H575 L68 2003
    813′.54—dc21   2002028422

Though my heroine, with her peanut
butter and pickle sandwiches,
isn't much of a cook,
I'd like to dedicate this book
to my Aunt Mae, the best cook I know.

Prologue

"I want you to find a woman for me."

Grady Chapman leaned easily against the massive desk in the colonel's library and grinned. "Can't you find one on your own?"

Folding beefy arms across a bulldog chest, Trevor Tyson frowned at the younger man. "Not just any woman. A particular one."

"Business?"

"It's personal."

"Why me?"

"Because you're the best there is." The older man hunched over his desk. "If I could do it myself, I would. But I can't, and there's no one else I trust enough."

A troubleshooter for Tyson Industries for over a decade, Grady was used to dealing with problems affecting the various businesses that comprised the Tyson empire, but he had never before been asked to run interference in his boss's personal life. He wasn't even sure the old man had a personal life, outside of his sister.

"What's so special about it? Why can't

one of your regular people handle it?"

"It's personal," Tyson repeated. "You're the only one I trust to handle it."

"What else?"

"That's it."

Grady raised an eyebrow. Tyson was lying. Grady knew it. What's more, Tyson knew Grady knew it.

Tyson shifted his gaze away from Grady and coughed. "Well, what are you waiting for?"

"The truth."

"I want her found. That's the only truth you need to know."

Grady waited. The colonel was used to calling the shots, and usually Grady let him. He wasn't into power trips; he left those to the people who needed them. He'd learned a long time ago that patience often netted more than arguing ever achieved.

Tyson gave a disgruntled *harrumph*. "You're an arrogant cuss, you know that?"

Silently, Grady counted to ten. It was a trick he'd picked up in the Marines. It stood him in good stead then, and now.

The colonel sighed. "I have reason to believe she's my niece."

"Your niece?"

"That's right. Laura's child."

Grady tried to make sense of that. As far as he knew, the colonel's sister had never been married, never had any children. "You might as well tell me the rest of it."

"That's it." Tyson grunted when Grady made no comment. "Twenty-eight years ago, Laura made a fool of herself over a man. He left her. Just like I predicted. She had the child and put it up for adoption."

"Why?" From what he knew of Laura Tyson, she didn't seem the kind of woman who'd give up her child.

Impatience glimmered in Tyson's eyes. "She wasn't married."

"Lots of unmarried women keep their children. Even twenty-eight years ago."

"Not Laura."

Not a Tyson, Grady translated silently.

"I pointed out the advantages of putting the child up for adoption."

"What did Laura want?"

"She wanted to keep the kid. Said she didn't care what people thought. I reminded her she had a responsibility to the family not to drag the Tyson name through the mud."

A soft hiss escaped Grady's lips. He bit his lower lip almost savagely. Whatever her mistakes, no one deserved that kind of pressure heaped on her.

"So you forced her to give away her child."

"Laura listens to me."

Four words, but they said much. Trevor Tyson, Colonel, United States Marines, retired, expected total obedience.

When it came to conflict, Colonel Trevor Tyson had never in his life settled for anything less than total victory. Not in battle. Not in business. Certainly not now.

Something in the colonel's eyes, a look that said there was more to it than what he let on, caused Grady's gut to clench. He'd learned to trust that feeling. "I think I'll give this one a pass. Give it to Sanders," he said, naming one of Tyson's top men.

"You have an older brother, don't you? David. Served in 'Nam."

"So?" The abrupt change of subject increased Grady's wariness.

"A certain letter's come into my possession . . . a letter concerning your brother. Perhaps you'd like to read it."

Grady took the much-folded letter and scanned it. His lips tightened as he read it once more. "It's nothing but a bunch of lies."

"You're sure about that?"

"Of course . . ." He paused.

David had never talked much about that

time. Grady had always chalked up David's reluctance to a natural desire to avoid any reminder of the war, a war that had cost him his legs. He never even displayed the medal of bravery he'd received, preferring to keep it hidden away.

"You don't believe me. Maybe you'll believe these." Tyson thrust a sheaf of papers into Grady's hands.

Scanning them, he saw they backed up the letter.

"Why not call your brother?"

Grady started to reach for the phone when he stopped. "Alone."

"As you say." Tyson let himself out of his library through the double doors. Ten minutes later, he reappeared. "Finished?"

"Where do I start?"

The satisfied smirk on Tyson's lips rasped against Grady's already frayed nerves.

"Glad you see it my way."

Chapter One

It hadn't taken long.

"I've found her," Grady stated with no preliminaries. Seated in the library, he was careful to keep his face blank. From past experience he knew little escaped the colonel's notice.

"It didn't take you long."

"No," Grady agreed, "it didn't."

"Where?"

"Colorado — a little town outside of Colorado Springs."

"What's she doing?"

"She owns a construction business that specializes in restoring old houses."

Tyson placed his fingers together steeplefashion. "Anything else?"

"She was adopted when she was a few months old. The couple returned her when she turned two. Said they'd made a mistake. She spent the next eight years in foster homes before a couple named Jameson adopted her. They moved to Colorado shortly after that."

Grady felt a swift stab of sympathy for the little girl who'd been shuffled back and forth for almost ten years. "She's well liked and respected in the community. Her business is small but growing." He studied Tyson before asking the question that had been on his mind since the older man had blackmailed him into taking the job.

"When are you going to tell Laura?"

The colonel frowned. "I hired you to do a job, not ask questions about things that are none of your business."

Neat evasion — counter with an attack. Grady shouldn't have been surprised. The colonel had used the tactic enough while in the military.

Tyson lowered his gaze. A twitch of his jaw muscles exposed his displeasure — and something more.

"Well, what are you waiting for?"

"What?" Still immersed in his own thoughts, Grady stared blankly at him.

"Get close to her, find out what she's like."

"I told you. She owns her own business. She's well liked, respected."

Tyson snapped his fingers. "That's nothing. I want to know what makes her tick. If she needs money. What's she willing to do to get it."

"Why?"

"Because that's why I'm paying you." A

13

large vein in his neck bulged, betraying his annoyance.

"Correction: you blackmailed me into finding her. Nothing less, nothing more."

"You like Laura, don't you?"

The question took Grady by surprise. He had a soft spot for the colonel's sister. Quiet, fragile-looking Laura Tyson was the opposite of her brother in every respect. He'd talked with her casually over the years, liking her quick wit and gentle manners. Stricken with rheumatoid arthritis early in life, Laura stayed close to home.

"If it weren't for Laura's health," Tyson said, rubbing his cheek reflectively, "I wouldn't be so concerned. But she's fragile. Especially now. I don't want to see her hurt."

"Why now? Why do you want to find her daughter after all these years?"

"I don't." The colonel looked irritated. "It's Laura. She's got some fool notion she wants to see her child. I tried to tell her she doesn't know what kind of can of worms she's opening up, but she can be mighty stubborn when she wants to."

"It might be good for her to see her daughter. Didn't you say Laura's been depressed lately? I think —"

"You're not paid to think. You're paid to

get results. I don't want Laura involved. I told her I'd take care of it and that's what I intend to do."

Grady stared at the man who had been first his commander and then his boss for over a decade. His gaze was unwavering.

"You wanted to say something?" Tyson asked.

"Yeah." With a casualness that belied his inner tension, Grady leaned back in his seat. "*If* I go back, it will be on my own terms. I'll find out what you want, but I do it my way."

Tyson gave him a measuring look.

Grady returned it with one of his own. Cold gray eyes clashed with brown.

The colonel was the first to look away.

Stephanie Jameson ran her fingers through her hair impatiently.

"Just what we need," she muttered to herself. "One less man on a project that's already behind schedule."

Bill Riedman had up and quit that day. He'd given no explanation, just said he had to be moving on. She shook her head, sending the already tousled curls into further abandon.

She went over the figures once more. If they fell behind another week, they'd not only lose the bonus Mrs. Patterson had promised, they'd have to pay a penalty as well.

Legacies Construction couldn't afford the latter. And a bonus, Stephanie admitted, would go a long way in helping to pay off the bank loan she'd taken out last year. For the first time, Legacies was showing a profit, a small but steadily growing profit. She aimed to keep it that way.

A knock at the door of the small trailer she used for an office and on-site living quarters interrupted her thoughts. The door was pushed open as she called, "Come in."

She smiled at Hank Caruthers, her foreman. Hank had thinning hair, the beginnings of a paunch, and a perpetual grin. He'd been with her father when he started the company twenty years ago. Today, the grin was conspicuously absent.

"Hey, boss, got a minute?"

"Sure, Hank. What's up?"

"The crew's —" He cleared his throat. "We're all sort of wondering if you're gonna hire another man. Everyone's already pulling ten-hour days as it is. Without Riedman, it looks like we're gonna have to work around the clock to meet the deadline."

16

Stephanie sighed. "I know, Hank. Tell them I'm working on it, okay?"

"Okay." He paused, shuffling from one foot to the other, a sure sign he was unhappy with what he had to tell her.

"Is there something else?" she asked gently.

"It's Cathy," Hank said, naming his wife. "She's after me to take a job with one of the big outfits. It's not just the salary. They've got benefits, insurance . . ."

Stephanie resisted the urge to indulge in a good cry. Hank Caruthers was not only her foreman, he was her best friend. If he quit, she'd be lost in more ways than one.

"It's not that I don't like working here," he said. "It's just with the baby coming and all. . . ." He lifted his hands, a silent gesture of appeal. "Cathy feels real bad about this, almost as bad as I do. But she says we gotta think about the baby."

"I know," Stephanie said, struggling to keep the dismay from her voice. "I don't blame you for wanting to work for a bigger outfit. I can't match them in wages or benefits." *And probably never will be able to,* she added to herself.

Hank had married late in life to a woman half his age. Proving the doomsayers wrong, Hank and Cathy appeared blissfully happy, especially since they'd learned they were expecting.

"If it was just me, I'd stick with you. For the first time in a long time, I feel good about what I'm doing. Your pa was a good man but . . ."

Stephanie nodded. After the death of her mother, her father had let things go.

"Yeah, well, things are good here now. The other companies out there throw up a place in a week, slap on some paint, and hope no one notices it's falling down about their ears till the ink on the contract's dry."

"I know," she said ruefully. At her father's insistence, she'd apprenticed at several such places. Nothing but the very cheapest was their motto. She'd resisted at first, telling him she didn't need to work for other outfits when all she wanted was to join him in the business, but he'd held firm. Now she was glad for the experience. She'd come to appreciate her dad's commitment to quality.

"I'll stick around for as long as I can. I just thought I ought to tell you for when —" He patted her awkwardly on the shoulder. "Just thought I ought to tell you."

"I appreciate it," she said around the lump in her throat. She waited until he let himself out before she let her shoulders droop into a defeated slump.

She didn't blame Hank. He had a wife to think of, a baby on the way. If he could do better with another company, she wouldn't stand in his way.

"Leave tomorrow's trouble for tomorrow," her mother had said often enough. That was just what Stephanie intended to do. She didn't need to go borrowing tomorrow's troubles. Right now, she had enough of today's.

Impatient with her ruminations, she pushed her chair back and stood. Her shoulders ached from the long hours at her desk. She smiled suddenly, acknowledging to herself that she didn't notice any discomfort when she was bent over a piece of wood, measuring and cutting.

She wasn't cut out for the paperwork end of owning a business. Someday, she promised herself, someday, she'd hire an accountant and *he* could handle the business end of things. Until then, she'd just have to deal with it herself.

Outside, she watched as her crew went about the business of reconstructing the porch that would wrap around the front and side of the house. She intended to fabricate the gingerbread-trim scalloping on the porch roof herself.

She liked the smell, the feel of working with wood — the aroma of fresh wood shavings, the texture of the grain beneath her fingers. She even liked the sounds. The whine of a power saw, the steady ping of a hammer, the rumble of lumber when it crashed to the ground — she loved them all.

The Patterson mansion was going to be a masterpiece of Victorian style when Legacies was finished with it. Sally Patterson had told Stephanie she wanted every detail authentic, right down to the specially designed bannister that Stephanie had carved. The old Patterson mansion had been built in the late 1800s. But a decline in the family fortunes and years of neglect had seen it deteriorate into its present state.

Stephanie had known when she bid on the project that it wasn't going to be easy. But she'd wanted the restoration job. Not only would it be a showplace to advertise Legacies, it was also an opportunity to bring to life a piece of the past.

She knew the men on the crew made jokes about her preoccupation with the past. She took it good-naturedly. After all, she was the first to admit she loved old houses. They were a part of history, a connection between the past and the present. If she had her way, they'd be part of the future also.

Perhaps her concern with the past was natural, she mused. A child who'd grown up in foster homes, only to be adopted later in life, she had more reason than most to be interested in the past. She had no roots of her own. Maybe this was her way of making up for it.

The old Patterson house was special. She'd felt a connectedness to it immediately. Maybe it was the lack of care it had received, the decay, that drew her to it. She'd been much the same until the Jamesons had adopted her. She too had been waiting. Waiting for someone to notice her, to care for her, to love her. Sarah and Ron Jameson had nourished talents she wasn't even aware of, praising her when she succeeded, encouraging her when she failed. She'd waited nearly eleven years to find someone to love her.

The old house had waited far longer than that. If she had her way, though, it wouldn't wait much longer. Her thoughts led her back to where she'd started. What she needed right now was a first-rate finish carpenter. But the chances of finding one in Bozeman at this late date were slim to none.

"Hey, boss."

She turned to see Hank walking toward her, a tall, brown-haired man at his side. He carried himself easily, with the kind of grace that said he was comfortable with who — and what — he was. It was only when he moved nearer that she saw something in his eyes, a shadow of pain that struck a chord within her.

"I think we might have a replacement for Bill," Hank said.

"Grady Chapman, ma'am." The stranger stuck out his hand.

She took it, liking the feel of his handshake. It was firm, without being hard, gripping hers with a quiet strength that said he had no need to impress anyone. Her fingers encountered ridged calluses. "Stephanie Jameson."

She took her time studying him. He had the lean, tough muscles of a man accustomed to hard work. Resisting the urge to fidget under his assessing look, she waited while he completed his own inspection.

"Grady here says he's looking for work," Hank put in when the silence between them stretched.

22

"What kind of work do you do?" she asked.

"A little bit of everything." Brown eyes, the color of melted chocolate, squinted at the sun's reflection. "But given my choice, I prefer carpentry."

She shaded her own eyes against the glare of the sun and stared up at him. Since he must have topped six feet, it was a long way. "You know your way around tools?"

"You could say that." A faint smile chased across his lips.

"It's what you say that matters."

"Yeah." His smile deepened, a slow, chipped-tooth smile that did funny things to her insides. "I know my way around tools."

It was too much to hope for, but she asked it anyway. "You ever do any finish carpentry?"

He rocked back on the heels of his cowboy boots, thumbs hooked in the pockets of his much-worn jeans. "Matter of fact, I've done a bit. It's been a while, though."

She couldn't believe her luck. "I'll show you what we're doing." She headed to the house. When he didn't follow, she called over her shoulder, "Coming?"

The house was in the worst shape of any he'd ever encountered. Rotting timbers, mildew-damaged woodwork, and cracked plaster were just the beginning.

"Pretty bad, huh?" she asked, gesturing around.

"You must be partial to understatements."

"We're going to change all that." Her eyes grew dreamy. "Can't you just see it all fixed up the way it was meant to be? Velvet settees in the parlor, a walnut sideboard in the dining room, pictures of stern-faced ancestors hanging on the walls."

It was a stretch for his imagination to see what she obviously pictured so effortlessly. But looking at Stephanie and seeing the excitement in her eyes, he caught a glimpse of the vision of restoring the mansion to its former glory.

"Ever do any fancy carving?" she asked.

"You mean like that?" He gestured toward the elaborately carved bannister and ran his hand over the wood. It was a beautiful piece in walnut. The workmanship was the finest he'd ever seen, the detail exquisite. He whistled in appreciation. "Yours?"

She nodded, her cheeks flushed.

"It's beautiful."

Her face glowed with pleasure. "I had a beautiful piece of wood to work with."

He traced the grain of the wood. It was smooth, almost satiny, to the touch. "I can see that. I can also see what you did with it. Where'd you learn to do work like that?"

"My dad taught me."

He liked the way she said "my dad." Not "my adopted father," but "my dad."

"Was the original bannister destroyed?"

"Yes. The customer showed me a picture of it, and I copied it."

"I'd say he got a good deal."

"It's a she. And I got lucky. Woodwork is difficult, if not impossible, to duplicate. That takes time and money. Fortunately, the owner has both."

Grady studied the bannister. It must have taken weeks to complete. Plus a good deal of patience. He looked at Stephanie Jameson with new respect. The lady gave her best — no stinting or cutting corners for her.

"We try to save as much of the original woodwork as we can," she said, pointing to the intricately carved moldings around the ceiling and the hardwood paneled doors. Somehow, they'd survived the years of neglect and would be as good as new once

25

they were stripped of their present coat of paint. "We reuse everything we can in restoration projects."

"Sounds good," Grady said, impressed by her common-sense approach.

"Our object is to maintain the original atmosphere of the house. I know a lot of contractors believe it's better, not to mention easier, to level the whole structure and start fresh. That's not our attitude at Legacies." She gave him a long look. "What do you think? Can you work with us?"

"I'd like to try."

"How soon can you start?"

"Today soon enough?"

For the first time, she smiled. "Tomorrow will be fine. Take today to get settled. There's a rooming house not far from here. The food's good, the sheets are clean, and the rent's cheap."

He grinned, the crow's feet at the corners of his eyes deepening. "Sounds good."

Now that the preliminaries were over, Grady took his time in studying Stephanie Jameson. Hair that reminded him of the color of autumn leaves framed a heart-shaped face. Her green eyes held intelligence and humor.

Her jeans and blue work shirt were

stained and dusty, her hands slightly callused. A slight sheen of perspiration gave her face a glow.

The lady was no straw boss. He liked it that she wasn't afraid to get her hands dirty. The women he'd dated wouldn't know the difference between a hammer and a saw. He'd bet that Stephanie not only knew the difference, she'd know how to use them.

"You're staring," she said.

Caught, he smiled. "Was I? Sorry. I was just wondering how a woman came to be owner of a construction company."

"It's the nineties," she reminded him with a small shrug. "Women can do anything they want."

"I know. But it's still unusual."

"Not very. My father owned the company. When he died, I inherited it."

He knew there was more to it than that. His reports showed her adopted father had left her a rundown company with little or no assets and a mountain of debts. The little he'd learned so far about Legacies revealed it was well run, respected in the local business community, and operating in the black with only one outstanding loan. Not bad for a small business. Not bad at all. His respect for the lady went up another notch.

"Eight o'clock tomorrow morning then," she said as she started to walk away.

"Ms. Jameson?" he called.

She turned.

"Thanks for the job. You won't be sorry you took me on."

"It's Stephanie, and you're welcome." She fixed him with a steady gaze. "I hope you're right."

It wouldn't be any hardship working here, he decided. From what he'd seen of the operation so far, it was first class all the way despite its small size. He was impressed — with Legacies and with its owner.

Grady watched as she headed back to the construction site. She walked with unstudied grace, making him think of a dancer. With a start, he realized who she reminded him of. Laura Tyson. A younger, happier Laura.

Forcibly, he jerked his thoughts back to the job he was here to do. He walked back to his truck, a frown replacing his earlier grin. He didn't like deceiving Stephanie. One look at her eyes convinced him she was as honest and open as the Colorado sky.

Right now, though, he didn't like his job

very much. In fact, he didn't much like himself.

Then he thought of David. He owed his brother. Big time. There was no way he'd let Tyson get his claws into him.

Chapter Two

Stephanie pushed back her hair and sighed. Balancing a checkbook would never come first on her list of fun things to do. But the figures had come out right. For once.

That was the good news.

The bad news was that the balance in the company account was precariously low.

Another good year, maybe two, and she'd be out of the woods. The bank loan would be whittled down to a more manageable size, and she might even be able to afford some new equipment. Unfortunately, the construction business wasn't known for its stability. Feast or famine seemed to be the motto.

Her dad had bet everything he had on the boom in the eighties. When the recession set in, he'd found himself overextended. He'd never managed to pull himself out of the quagmire of bills and debt.

Straightening her shoulders, she focused on the positive. Legacies was showing a profit and establishing a small but growing reputation. If she completed the Patterson project on schedule, she could count on a good recommendation from Mrs. Patterson. One of the social leaders in the town, Sally Patterson carried a lot of influence. A word from her could make a company's reputation . . . or break it.

In addition, she had another job, a referral from a satisfied client. The only problem was time. Perhaps if she pulled some men off the Patterson job. . . .

She pushed her chair back from her makeshift desk, an old door stretched across two filing cabinets. Coffee stains, scratches, and blueprint ink covered its surface. It wasn't much to look at, but it was practical. What was more, it had cost her nothing, a prime factor, considering the current state of her finances.

She wondered about the new man who'd shown up on the site that day. With Bill Riedman leaving without a word, she was seriously shorthanded. Grady Chapman was heaven sent. If he worked out like she hoped, she'd offer him a permanent job.

She frowned. He didn't look like the kind of man who stayed in one place for very long. A drifter? Maybe. But somehow she didn't think so.

Perhaps it was in the way he had of looking at a person with eyes so steady and

31

clear that you knew he was someone you could count on. Perhaps it was the respectful, almost reverent way he had of touching a piece of wood. Only a few people possessed that quality, that special affinity with the wood. Her dad was one of them. Hank was another. And now Grady.

Over the following days, she kept a close watch on Chapman. He kept to himself for the most part, working quietly and methodically at any job assigned him.

When she needed an extra pair of hands to steady the trim she was scrolling to place above the front entryway, he volunteered. They were so close that she could smell the spicy scent of his aftershave. His fingers accidentally brushed hers as they reached to steady the piece of wood at the same time.

She snatched her hand away and then flushed. There was no need to feel flustered, no reason for the tingling awareness that shivered up her arm. Still, she couldn't stem the color that she knew was flooding her face.

"Thanks," she said when they completed the job.

"No problem."

"You . . . uh . . . you're very good."

He gestured to the carved bannister.

"I've got something to live up to."

Pleasure at his words heightened the color in her already-pink cheeks.

"Stephanie, you got a moment?" Hank looked uncertainly from her to Grady. "Sorry. I didn't know you were busy."

"I'm not," she said. "What do you need?"

"The delivery's here. You said you wanted to check it before we signed for it."

"The delivery . . ." Her mind was fuzzy, and she shook her head to clear it. "Thanks, Hank." With a nod to Grady, she followed her foreman outside.

She checked the order and signed the invoice, conscious all the while of Hank's quizzical gaze. It wasn't like her to forget anything, much less something as important as a thousand-dollar shipment.

"You okay, boss?" Hank asked, once they were alone.

"I'm fine. I've just got a lot on my mind."

"Yeah," he said, but his voice lacked conviction.

For the rest of the day, she was careful to keep her distance from Grady. She couldn't afford the kind of distraction he offered.

She'd known Grady Chapman less than seventy-two hours and already he was occupying far too much of her thoughts. Determined to put him out of her mind, she returned her attention to the job.

"Need some help there?" Grady asked.

She looked down at the corner she was mitering. Truth was, she could use an extra hand, but remembering her resolve, she shook her head. "No . . . thanks."

Grady let his gaze rest on her for a few more moments before walking away. He had an idea why Stephanie had refused his offer of help. She was scared. Over the last few days, he'd noticed that while she was friendly with the members of her crew, she kept her distance. Only with Hank did she let her guard down.

Now he wondered about her reaction to him. Did she share the attraction he felt for her? The idea pleased him until he realized its implications. He'd do well to remember that he was here to do a job, and concentrate his energies on that.

When quitting time came, Stephanie gave an absent wave to the men as they left.

"You staying on?" Hank asked.

"I thought I'd finish framing this door," she said, not looking up from where she measured a strip of trim.

"I'll give you a hand."

She lifted her head. "And risk having Cathy yell at me for keeping you late? No way. You get home and take care of her."

"You sure?"

She assumed a fierce glare. "I'm still the boss around here, aren't I?"

He grinned. "Yes, ma'am."

A matching grin curved her lips. "Just so you remember."

When she heard his retreating footsteps, she pulled an orange soda from an ice chest, popped the lid, and drank deeply. Orange had been her father's favorite. The memory of him no longer gave her pain as it once had, and she found herself smiling as she thought of how he'd buy a case of it at a time.

"Any more where that came from?" a voice asked.

Startled, she spun around.

"Sorry," Grady said. "I didn't mean to scare you."

"It's all right. I just didn't expect . . . I thought everyone had gone." She tossed him a can.

He caught it easily and flipped open the lid. "I've got no place I have to be. Figured I'd stay and see if you needed some help."

She hesitated. Having another pair of hands would make the work go a lot faster.

What of her determination to keep her distance, though?

"Hey, if it makes you uncomfortable or something, just say so and I'll get out of here."

She watched as he tipped back the can and took a long drink. "No," she said quickly, feeling foolish. She drained the last of her soda and tossed the can in a corner where several others were piled. "I'd appreciate the help."

He finished his off as well. "I saw you chase Hank off," he said as he held a piece of trim in place while she nailed it. "He'd have stayed if you'd asked him to."

"Yeah."

"Why didn't you?"

"Because he'd have stayed." At the question in his eyes, she said, "He has a wife and a baby on the way." A wrinkle worked its way between her brows as she measured the next piece.

"You care about him."

It wasn't a question, and she didn't treat it as such. "Hank's my best friend. He'd do anything for me. That's why I can't ask him."

Grady nodded, as if confirming something to himself.

They worked well together, quickly establishing a rhythm of measuring, sawing, and nailing.

The hours passed quickly, melting away under Grady's undemanding company. He regaled her with stories about other construction sites he'd worked on. Any doubts she had concerning his experience vanished as she watched the comfortable way he handled tools.

Not that he was casual with them. He was too much a professional for that. He treated his tools with a care and respect that she had to admire.

The job, which would have taken her half the night by herself, was done shortly before eleven. She watched as he cleaned his tools, wiping them carefully with a soft cloth until they gleamed. A man who paid that kind of attention to his tools was likely to give the same attention to his work.

"Mind if I ask you a personal question?" he asked as he made himself comfortable on the tarp that covered the floor. He patted the place beside him, and after a moment's hesitation, she sat down beside him.

"If I do, I'll let you know."

"Why do you keep yourself distant from the rest of the crew?"

She stiffened. "Do I?"

"Yeah. You're friendly, but only up to a point. Then you back away. Just like you did this afternoon, with me."

"I didn't —"

His steady gaze silenced the lie she'd been about to utter. "Okay, so maybe I did."

"Why?" he asked bluntly.

"I was never very good at making friends."

"Then we have something in common."

To her relief, he didn't pursue the subject. They resumed their work, finishing just before eleven.

She slid her back down a wall and wrapped her arms around her knees. "Thanks. You saved me a late night."

"You're welcome." He stretched out. "You don't give yourself much slack, do you?"

"Can't afford to."

"Don't you ever take a day off?"

Her lips edged upward. "Sure. When the job's done, I may have a whole bunch of days off. Unscheduled days off, if you get my meaning."

He frowned. "You know what I mean."

Her smile died. "Yeah. Right now, though, I can't afford a day off. Not if I want to make my next payment to the bank."

"You push yourself too hard."

A lazy smile touched her lips. "My boss is a hard case."

"Yeah. She's a real slave driver, all right."

Drowsily, she tried to focus on what he was saying. She felt her eyes close and tried to force them open, but it was too much effort.

"Stephanie?"

"Mmm."

Something shook her shoulder. She shrugged it off. She felt strong arms lifting, carrying her. Of course it was a dream. She knew where she was. In a few minutes, she'd get up and head to her trailer. In the meantime, though, she'd enjoy the sensation of being held against a hard chest.

The dream was alive with details. A breeze whispered over her. She heard a door opening, then closing. Now she nestled into her bed, and felt her shoes being removed and the covers being drawn over her.

"Sleep well," a voice murmured.

When pale streams of light found their way through the slatted windows of her trailer, she groaned and turned over, pulling the pillow over her head.

She peeked out at her alarm clock and

confirmed what she already knew. It was past time she was up, when all she wanted to do was crawl back under the covers and stay in bed for the rest of the day.

Bed.

She didn't remember going to bed last night. In fact, she didn't remember much of anything, beside the fact that she and Grady had finished framing the door.

Grady!

Had he brought her to the trailer and put her to bed? She roused herself enough to note that her jeans and work shirt were still intact, her shoes placed neatly beside the bed.

Her face heated with the memory of what she'd thought had been a dream — Grady lifting her, carrying her. Now she knew why it had seemed so real.

The man had seen a need and taken care of it. Nothing to get upset about. He probably hadn't given it a second thought. Well, neither would she.

Only one flaw marred her resolve. The memory of those strong arms holding her close refused to vanish.

Work filled the following days. She dropped into bed at night exhausted but happy. The Patterson job was moving along at a rate she had only dared to hope for. Part of the reason — a large part, she acknowledged — was Grady. There was nothing he couldn't turn his hand to.

He'd quickly made friends among the crew. Only Hank remained unconvinced about him.

When Stephanie asked her foreman about it, he gave her a noncommittal smile. "The jury's still out on Chapman."

His stubborn refusal to accept Grady as part of the team puzzled her. Still, she couldn't order the men to like one another. As long as they were willing to work together, she wouldn't complain.

"I'm thinking of pulling you and Richards and Howe off this project and sending you over to the Conrad place," she said Monday morning. "I'd feel better if we got a head start on that."

Hank looked surprised. "What about the deadline? I thought the Patterson job had top priority."

"It does. But that doesn't mean I can afford to tie up the whole crew on it."

Her foreman scratched his head. "Who you going to leave here?"

"Chapman and Thompson."

He hesitated. "What about you?"

"I'll be staying on here. This is my baby," she said, glancing fondly about.

Hank grinned. "Yeah. Don't I know it." His grin faded, worry lines working their way across his forehead. "You sure about Chapman? I know the guy knows his way around tools, but he's still pretty new. You don't know him."

"I know enough. Why don't you trust him?"

"I don't *not* trust him. That don't mean I trust him, if you get my meaning."

Stephanie got it, all right. And didn't like it. "Has he done anything to make you distrust him?"

"No. . . ." Hank drew the word out. "But something doesn't sit right with me. Chapman's no ordinary carpenter."

She smiled, relieved. "You're right about that. He's the best finish carpenter I've ever seen."

"Yeah. But that ain't what I meant."

Exasperated now, she squared her hands on her hips. "Just what do you mean?"

"He's a fine craftsman. Mighty fine. So why's he working for . . ." His voice trailed off in an embarrassed silence.

"A small-potatoes outfit like Legacies," she finished for him.

"You run a first-class place," Hank said quickly. "You know that. But I can't help wondering about Chapman. He could name his own price, but he picks here."

She'd wondered the same thing. Right now, though, she needed him too much to question her good luck in his turning up. "Anything else bothering you?"

Hank shook his head. "Don't mind me. I'm just looking out for you, the way your pa would have wanted me to."

"I appreciate it."

And she did. Hank was the closest thing she had to a family. He didn't have much formal education, but he had more people smarts than anyone she knew. If he said something didn't seem right about Grady Chapman, she ought to listen.

For the first time she could remember, she ignored Hank's advice. She did need Grady if she were going to finish the job on time, but honesty compelled her to admit it was more than that.

She liked him.

She shoved her hair back from her forehead and laughed at herself. Since when had she started thinking of herself as Cinderella and Grady as some kind of Prince Charming? He'd probably be embarrassed to death if he learned of her fantasies.

So, she was attracted to the man. That wasn't hard to understand. Aside from being the best-looking man she'd come across in ages, Grady was also intelligent and sensitive. She had the feeling that he'd understand what she wanted to do with Legacies, her need to make it a success.

By six that evening, she was ready to call it a day. The rest of the crew had already left. Switching off the power saw, she started to clean up when she heard footsteps on the floor above.

More exasperated than concerned, she picked her way over the debris and headed upstairs. It was probably just Hank, trying to get a head start on tomorrow's work. She'd chew him out and send him on his way. She knew he was worried about making the schedule, but she couldn't allow him to work evenings as well as days. Cathy'd have her hide.

The lecture she planned to deliver was forgotten as she saw Grady holding a wall of two-by-fours in place. She didn't bother with words but raised one side of it while he held the other.

"A few more steps," Stephanie said, "and we'll have it."

"Yeah." Grady let out the word in a grunt of effort while balancing his side of a framed wall. He had to admire Stephanie's skill. She couldn't have weighed over one

44

hundred and ten pounds, but she managed to hold up her side without straining. She knew how to lift, using her legs instead of her back.

She used the level, adjusting the angle of the wall slightly. "Ready."

Grady nailed the bottom plate with a nail gun, moved the stepladder, and repeated the process with the top plate, nailing it to the ceiling. The new wall formed the doorway into what would be a huge bathroom, complete with hot tub and his-and-her vanities.

"Look, I appreciate your staying late to finish up, but I can't let you keep doing it. I can't afford the overtime," Stephanie said regretfully.

"I'm not looking for overtime."

"What then?"

"Just trying to get the job done."

"I appreciate it," she said. "But it's not right. You put in an eight-hour day as it is."

"Hey, I like doing it. Are you going to dock a guy for liking his work?"

Put like that, she couldn't very well object. "Okay." Realizing how ungracious she must have sounded, she smiled. "I really do appreciate it."

"No problem." He seemed anxious to drop the subject. "This is going to be some place," he said, unable to keep a trace of envy from his voice. When had he started caring about — or even noticing — houses? His condominium served one purpose: a place for him to crash between jobs. That was all he ever needed, or wanted, up until now.

"When it's done," she said. "Which I hope is real soon."

"You're not getting tired of the job already, are you?"

She shook her head. "No way. This is a dream job. But I've got bids out for two more jobs. If we get them . . . Well, let's just say a lot of Legacies' money problems would be solved. But I've got to get this one out of the way first."

"We'll make it," he said, brushing a smudge of dust from her cheek. "I promise."

"I'll hold you to that." She started back down the stairway. "By the way, I'm thinking of sending the rest of the crew over to the Conrad place."

"Everyone?"

"Everyone but you, me, and Thompson. He's the best when it comes to drywall. You and I can take care of the woodwork. I think between us we can finish up the interior work."

"You're the boss."

The easy camaraderie between them suffused her with warmth as she undressed for bed that night. Grady Chapman was fast becoming important to her. Maybe too important.

She clamped down on the idea with a determination that surprised her. She was twenty-eight years old, after all. If she found a man attractive, and the feeling was mutual, why shouldn't she act on it?

"C'mon," she said to the object of her thoughts the following morning. "We've still got a bathroom to finish framing."

"Slave driver," Grady called. "There are laws against overworking your employees, you know."

"Yeah? Take up it with the union."

He laughed, liking her quick sense of humor almost as much as he liked the way she looked in a pair of jeans.

They finished roughing in the framing of the bathroom by noon. Grady had to hand it to Stephanie. She worked her employees hard, but no harder than herself. She hefted a wall of two-by-fours with an ease that belied her small size.

While he pulled out a sandwich and thermos from his lunch box and settled down in the shade of a tree, she sat on the porch and pored over blueprints, eating yogurt from a carton. Every once in a while, he could hear her muttering to herself.

"Hey," he called. "Come on over and relax. You need a break."

"Can't," she called back. "I've got to go over these and get a bid ready."

"All work and no play makes Jill a dull girl," he quoted.

"All play and no work makes Jill a broke girl." She stood, planted her hands on her hips, and wagged a finger at him. "Lunchtime's over. Back to work."

He gave a mock salute. "Yes, ma'am. What's next?"

"The powder room."

"Powder room?"

"Don't tell me you're one of those men who've never heard of a powder room?"

"Oh, I've heard of it all right. I just thought it was a fancy name for a john."

"It's a place for ladies to powder their noses."

"They need a whole room for that?" He was teasing her. What's more, he liked it. He liked the way her cheeks flushed pink and her eyes widened as she tried to make him be serious.

"After we finish that," she said, "we convert the maid's room and bath into an efficiency apartment."

"Why do they need a separate apartment?"

A smile flirted at the corners of her mouth. "The husband's mother tends to make extended visits."

"Oh."

"Yeah. Oh."

He cocked his head to one side. "Of course, there are those who'd say building a whole apartment for her is the wrong way to go about discouraging her from visiting."

Stephanie laughed. "Sally's already figured that out. But she said Tim's mother will come no matter what, so they might as well have a place for her. A *separate* place."

She ticked off her fingers. "The kitchen next, then the bedroom upstairs, then —"

"Hold it. You've got enough work lined up for two teams, and you expect the three of us to do the whole job?"

"I'll pull some men off another job when we need them. But I'm hoping we can handle the next few days by ourselves."

He saw the worry in her eyes. "Are things that bad?"

"No . . . not really. Only I can't afford any more men right now."

"Listen, if it'd help, I don't need my paycheck this week. I can wait until things are better."

"That's really decent of you, Grady. But things aren't that bad. When it gets to where I can't pay my crew, it's time to close up."

"You're a special lady, Stephanie Jameson."

She smiled, though it had a forced quality to it. He frowned, wondering what was wrong.

"Did I say something out of line?"

"No . . . it's just my dad used to call me his 'little lady.' I haven't thought of that in over a year. Not since he died."

He touched her cheek. "I'm sorry. I didn't mean to bring back memories."

"Don't apologize. They're good memories. I keep them stored away so I can take them out and relive them." She laughed. "Sometimes I think I stored them away too much." She looked at him curiously. "Do you store away memories too?"

Grady thought about it and then nodded slowly. "I guess I do."

"Do you ever take them out and look at them again?"

"No." He didn't qualify his answer. Some memories hurt too much to examine. Better to let them stay buried.

"Oh." She bit her lip.

"Hey, it's okay," he said to cover the awkward silence.

He couldn't stem the tide of memories, though. Rather than fight them, he let them have their way.

When his mother had died, his father had retreated into a shell of his own. The family that had been his for a short six years was no longer. He and his brother David had quickly learned to fend for themselves. Their father was drunk more often than not. His salary from the docks where he'd worked for over twenty years now barely provided for food and rent, after he'd spent most of it on whiskey.

For more nights than he cared to remember, Grady and David had gone to bed hungry. He could still hear his own cries some nights when darkness closed around him, the memories returning like a bad dream to haunt him with undiminished power.

At seventeen, David was practically supporting Grady and himself with two paper routes and odd jobs he'd picked up around the neighborhood. He'd sworn they'd never be hungry again.

After David had graduated, he'd joined

the Marines, sending most of his pay home. Grady had a bad case of hero worship back then. When David had signed up, Grady could hardly wait until he was old enough to join.

Things changed when David came home minus his legs, but Grady never forgot his dream of being a Marine.

After he'd served in Grenada under Colonel Trevor Tyson, he'd been sent to other trouble spots. Two years after Grady had returned home, the colonel had found him and offered him a job. That had been ten years ago.

Since then, he'd discovered he was good at what he did. Nothing gave him more of a rush than going into a tense situation, defusing it, and restoring order. He'd advanced until he'd become the colonel's number-one troubleshooter, called in when no one else could get the job done.

Getting the job done. That was the bottom line. Now it had changed, though. Protecting David was the only thing that mattered. The only thing that *could* matter.

Chapter Three

Stephanie brushed his cheek, her hand soft and warm. It wasn't soft in the way of the pampered hands of the women he usually dated. Their hands had never known the calluses that came from hard work.

No, hers was soft in the way it touched his face, soft in the way it soothed away the pain of the past, soft in the way it gave comfort.

For those reasons . . . and more, Grady jerked away from it.

"I'm sorry," she murmured, flushing.

He tried a smile. "It's okay. You . . . startled me." He couldn't explain to her why he'd jumped as if he'd been scalded. She wouldn't understand. He wasn't sure *he* did.

Softness had no place in the memories he'd recalled just minutes ago. Softness had no place in his life at all. Then why did he respond with such startling intensity to the touch of a woman's hand? Especially *this* woman's hand? A woman he was sent to spy on.

As a child, his only means of survival

had been a strong body and a fierce determination. In the Marines, he'd honed his body and skills, ignoring the softer side of his nature.

Nothing in his life had prepared him to accept gentleness or compassion. So long had he been without them that he didn't know how to deal with them when they were offered. So he made it a rule to avoid them.

Oh, he had softer feelings. He wasn't the cold-blooded robot Tyson and others thought him. He'd deliberately cultivated that image, having found it useful in his line of work. But he'd learned early on to keep his more tender feelings under wraps. They made a man vulnerable, an emotion he couldn't afford.

Distance was the key word here. As long as he maintained a professional distance from Stephanie, he'd be all right.

With an effort, he brought himself back to the present. The harshness around his mouth disappeared, and he heard Stephanie draw a relieved breath.

He wiped his forehead with the back of his hand. It was so hot, he had stripped off his shirt. His chest and shoulders, bronzed brown by the sun, glistened under a fine sheen of sweat.

Stephanie couldn't help but notice his hard muscles, and she flushed as she realized that his eyes had followed the direction of her gaze.

When he turned back to her, she saw it. A thin scar ran from under his arm to disappear beneath the waistband of his jeans, a white slash against dark gold skin. She wanted to ask him about it but thought better of it. Another scar bisected his shoulder.

Finished with his task, Grady picked up his shirt. "Hope you don't mind that I shed my shirt. It's hotter than a —" He grinned. "It's plenty hot."

"I don't mind," she said, still thinking about the scar. "Uh . . . I . . ."

"What?"

"Nothing."

"Would nothing be the scar you were staring at?"

"How did . . . how did you know?"

"I've lived with that little souvenir for over fifteen years. Let's just say I'm accustomed to people's reactions."

There was nothing she could say to that. "I'm sorry."

"For staring?"

She shook her head. "That you were hurt."

His gaze bored into her until she flushed uncomfortably. "You really mean that, don't you?"

"Yes."

Her voice was but a thread of sound, but it must have registered for he nodded briefly.

Tentatively, she reached out. When he didn't flinch, her wandering fingers found and paused at the scar on his shoulder. She felt him tremble beneath her touch and then go still. He was holding himself motionless, as though she were hurting him all over again. Reason told her she wasn't, she was making her exploration as gentle as possible, but she couldn't help the hiss of breath that escaped her lips as she brought her hand away.

He wouldn't have been surprised to find the scars had disappeared completely when she removed her hand, so soothing was her touch, so gentle her probing fingers. This woman gave comfort as easily as she breathed. Everything in him clamored that he take what she offered. At the same time, everything revolted against accepting it. He didn't deserve her compassion.

She turned questioning eyes up to his. "Was it bad?" *Stupid question,* she scolded herself. Of course it had been bad. She had only to look at the network of scars to know the wounds must have brought him close to death.

"Not really," he said dismissively. When she didn't accept that, he relented and added, "Some."

"Were you hurt more than once?"

He heard the concern in her voice, a concern she hadn't even tried to hide. Stephanie was too honest to hide what she felt behind a protective armor. He saw the pain in her eyes. The feeling it roused in him startled him. He'd expected to be annoyed; instead, he felt warmed. How long had it been since someone — anyone — had cared about him?

The answer came with cruel swiftness. No one but David cared whether he lived or died. It was a long time to live with the knowledge that it would hardly raise a ripple in the world if he died.

"A few times."

She gave an anguished sigh. Slowly, her hands traveled across the firm muscles of his lower back, finding two more scars. Tears gathered in her eyes at the thought of his suffering.

He touched a finger to the glistening wetness on her cheeks. "Don't cry for me, honey. It was a long time ago."

"But you were all alone."

"Not really. There were others." A contraction of pain twisted his face as he remembered his buddies who hadn't made it home.

"But no one who cared what happened to you," she guessed, remembering how alone he seemed.

"I was one of the lucky ones."

"Lucky," she scoffed.

"I was," he insisted, looking uncomfortable with her compassion. "I came home all in one piece, which is more than a lot of men did. More than my . . ." He didn't finish, even when she glanced at him, questions clear in her eyes.

"I wish there weren't any wars," she said at last when it became plain he didn't intend to complete whatever it was he'd been about to say.

He nodded shortly. "So do I. Okay if I use the hose to wash up?"

"Sure." She watched as he turned the hose on, the water sluicing over him.

She felt the pressure of tears build behind her eyes. Something about this man saddened her. It was more than the scars slashing his skin, a mute reminder of a painful past. It was the aloofness he withdrew into whenever she got too close.

Loneliness like that was painful to see. It touched her down to her very soul.

She sighed and shelved the thought. Perhaps she was all wrong about him. Maybe he kept to himself because he preferred it that way. She shook her head, remembering the bleakness in his eyes when he'd talked of his past. No, she wasn't mistaken. He wanted — he needed — someone capable of understanding, of caring about him.

A frisson of uneasiness ruffled her heart. There were so many things about him that she didn't know, even more that she didn't understand. Grady Chapman had more than his share of secrets, secrets he had no intention of sharing with her.

A shiver danced down her spine as a new thought came to her. What if one of those secrets concerned her?

Where had that thought come from? The result of an overactive imagination, she decided, her lips curving into a faint smile. Her dad had teased her about her imagination more than once.

Whatever brought Grady to Legacies, she could only be grateful for. Though he'd been here only a few days, he'd accomplished a great deal. They were ahead of schedule on the Patterson job. A few more weeks would see it finished. And then they'd celebrate.

Maybe she ought to plan a party before the job was completed. The crew deserved a reward for all their hard work. It wouldn't have to be anything fancy. Maybe a barbecue. Invite the wives and families. The idea took shape, and she began jotting down notes.

She suggested the idea to Hank when he drove over from the other work site.

He grinned broadly. "The men'll love it. When were you thinking of?"

"Saturday night."

"Uh, boss?"

"Hmm?"

"Can you afford this?"

"I can swing it. We'll keep things simple."

The news of a party boosted everyone's morale. Spirits were high by Saturday night.

She took extra care with her appearance, choosing a flowered sundress in place of her usual jeans and shirt. Rather than pulling her hair back in its customary ponytail, she left it loose. She toned down the dusting of freckles and deepened the color of her lips. After spritzing on cologne — a birthday present from her dad shortly before he died — she decided she was ready.

Would Grady like her in a dress? The question unnerved her. It had been a long time since she'd been concerned if a man found her attractive — not since her college days. And then the man had quickly lost interest when she'd refused to do his term paper for him.

Impatient with herself, she pushed the memories aside and headed outside.

For the first time in over a year, Stephanie felt the burden of owning and operating a business slip from her shoulders. She joined in the country line dancing and visited with the families of her crew, enjoying the heady feeling of a successful party. Knowing Grady's gaze followed her every movement didn't hurt either.

"Dance with me?" he asked when the music slowed to a dreamy love song.

Her stomach fluttered with uneasy anticipation as he slipped an arm around her waist and tucked one of her hands up against his chest.

She felt enfolded by him, enveloped in a sweet warmth that she'd never before experienced. Settling into his embrace, she gave herself up to the moment. The black velvet sky, spangled by stars, provided the perfect canopy as the night air cooled her over-heated skin.

Stephanie closed her eyes and lifted her lips to Grady's, silently asking him to kiss her. He hesitated for a moment, as if he were having second thoughts about what might happen.

When his lips grazed hers, she sighed her pleasure. The kiss was warm and tender. The yearning it kindled inside her caused her to stiffen before the gentle pressure of his arms encouraged her to relax.

The music stopped, but he continued to hold her. Imperceptibly, his hold tightened, bringing her closer to him until only a fraction of an inch separated them. What she read in his eyes thrilled and confused her in turn.

"Hey, boss, great party," Thompson called, startling her out of the spell the music and Grady's kiss had cast over her. She felt his hands drop away from her sides.

"Thanks." She turned back to Grady, but he was gone.

She looked for him, but he must have left the party early. Struggling against her disappointment, she joined in a square dance and tried to wipe the memory of the kiss from her mind.

It was easier to think about work, about Hank and Cathy's soon-to-be-born baby, about anything other than what had just happened. The distraction worked for a while until she was alone.

As she was drifting between wakefulness and sleep, she puzzled over her response to Grady. She'd shared kisses with men before, but none had touched her the way Grady's had. None had had her longing for more.

None had left her trembling.

Hours later, when the moon scattered silvery fingers of light across his room, Grady berated himself.

He ought to have his head examined. What had possessed him to kiss her, to hold her as he'd done? He wasn't given to making promises, even unspoken ones.

And with the touch of his lips to hers, he'd done just that.

Without effort, he conjured up Stephanie's image in his mind. Tall and slender, with a delicate bone structure, she reminded him of a fine thoroughbred. Her already pale skin, stretched tautly over her cheekbones, was made almost translucent against the burnished gold of her hair.

In spite of her fragile appearance, Grady sensed a hidden strength about her that told him she would meet whatever hardships she faced.

Resolutely, he put her out of his mind and tried to go to sleep. Two hours later, he gave it up, his thoughts continually straying to the woman who was fast becoming the most important thing in his life.

Why he should feel that way when he'd just met the woman baffled him. Repeatedly he told himself she wasn't his type.

Who are you trying to kid? He scoffed at himself. *You met her only a few days ago.* But he felt he'd known her far longer; she had been in his thoughts ever since he'd first seen her.

He couldn't shake his desire to wipe away the hurt that he read in her eyes, and spare her further pain. That he could be the instrument to inflict the pain tore at his insides with a gut-wrenching pang.

"Who are you, Stephanie?" he asked the silent night.

Suddenly his reason for being here sounded pretty thin. The woman who'd built up her own business, who cared about an out-of-work laborer, wasn't the type who should be spied upon.

Stephanie Jameson was an intriguing combination of independence and vulnerability, strength and compassion.

But he had no right to care about her, Grady reminded himself. He *couldn't* care.

He wondered whom he was trying to fool.

Grady and Stephanie had taken to sharing lunch. Thompson spent the noon hour with his girlfriend, leaving them alone. Grady had come to look forward to that time together.

In the shade of a huge mountain ash that flanked the house, she poked through the basket and pulled out a sandwich. "I don't know about you, but I'm starved."

He took the sandwich she offered him and bit into it. "Peanut butter and pickle?" It was all he could do to gag down the bite.

"Oops. That's mine. Here," she said, handing him the other sandwich. "It's peanut butter and jelly." She rolled her eyes. "Boring."

He took a cautious bite, relieved to find that it was what she claimed. "Boring can be good."

"That sounds like something a button-down type would say. Not you."

He supposed there was a compliment in there somewhere. "How'd you get hooked on peanut butter and pickles?" He peeled a banana and handed half to her.

"My dad. He used to make them by the dozen."

"How about your mom?"

"She was like you." Stephanie lowered her voice. "Can you believe it? She actually preferred jelly with her peanut butter!"

"Shocking."

Fun sparkled from her eyes. "Yeah, isn't it?"

Her laughter rippled over him, a soft caress of happiness that had been missing from his life for too long. So accustomed had he become to his solitary existence that he'd forgotten how good it felt simply to play.

His plan to get to know Stephanie better was backfiring. Everything he learned about her convinced him she was exactly what she appeared to be. Honest, hardworking, with a quirky sense of humor and a generous heart.

He had an ironclad rule about getting involved with anyone he met on the job. The rule had stood him in good stead through the years, and he had no intention of breaking it, never even been tempted to break it. Until now.

He knew better, but Stephanie Jameson tempted him as no woman had in more years than he cared to remember. Something about her had him thinking about white picket fences and home-cooked meals, a station wagon full of kids, and a tire swing hanging from a big shade tree.

Dreams he'd given up on long ago.

Strange how a woman could revive hopes he thought he'd buried another lifetime ago. Real strange.

But then he'd never met a woman like Stephanie, never felt this way before, never known it *could* be this way.

He reminded himself why he was here. As soon as he learned everything he could about Stephanie, the sooner he could leave and get back to his life.

Why did that life suddenly seem so empty? He ignored that and focused on the present.

"Tell me about what it was like growing up around here." He knew most of her history, but he wanted to hear it from her.

"I didn't."

He waited.

"I grew up in California. For the first ten years, I spent most of my time in foster homes. Some were good. Some not so good. I got used to being moved around every six months or so. I learned not to get too attached to any place or anyone. It was easier that way."

He listened to what she hadn't said as much as what she had. He pictured the solitary little girl, afraid to care too much, afraid to let herself get too attached to anyone, any place. He wanted to take her in his arms and wipe away all the hurt and loneliness.

"Then I was placed with the Jamesons. They were older and never had any kids of their own. I remember Mom — Mrs. Jameson — called me into the kitchen one day. I knew I was going to have to leave again. I was wrong. She told me they wanted to adopt me." Her voice softened in remembrance. "That was the happiest day of my life."

"How old were you then?" he asked, even though he knew the answer.

"Almost eleven. I'd given up hoping I'd be adopted a long time before that. Couples looking to adopt want babies, not skinny girls with scabs on their knees and freckles."

"I like freckles." To prove it, he kissed the tip of her nose.

"They were so good to me. They told me I was extra special because I was chosen." Her eyes took on a faraway look. "I wanted to believe them. And I did, after a while."

"But not at first?"

She shook her head. "I kept remembering the first couple who were going to adopt me. Right before it went through, they decided they didn't want me. They returned me, like some kind of defective goods."

Grady heard the hurt in her voice and ached for the child who'd been rejected, first by her own mother and then by others.

"They probably weren't cut out to be parents," he said. "Some people aren't."

"It turned out for the best. The Jamesons were wonderful to me. As soon as the adoption was final, we all went on a trip to Disneyland to celebrate." Her eyes grew misty. "We spent a week at a hotel. It was my first time.

"Mom died five years ago. Dad was never the same after that. He . . . he went last year. The doctor said it was a heart attack."

"You don't think so?"

A soft smile slipped across her lips. "I think he died of a broken heart."

"I'm sorry," he said, knowing how inadequate the words sounded and yet unable to say anything else.

"It's all right. I'm glad Dad and Mom

are together again. They weren't meant to be apart. They loved each other so much."

"And you."

She swiped at her eyes. "That's right. I have wonderful memories. That's more than some people ever have."

He brushed away a tear that had trickled down her cheek. "You still miss them."

"Yeah, I do." She shook off her melancholy. "What about you, Grady?"

Startled, he drew his hand away. "What about me?"

"What kind of memories do you have?"

He thought about it. There were good times, back before his mom died. Back when he had nothing more on his mind than getting together enough boys for a game of football.

"The regular kid memories." He shrugged. "Nothing special."

"Maybe someday you'll trust me enough to tell me."

"It's not that —"

She put a finger to his lips. "When you're ready, I'll be there."

He wondered if she knew what she was offering. If she'd be so willing to listen when it came time to tell her the truth about why he was here.

Bringing her hand to his lips, he kissed

her fingers, one by one.

She resisted the urge to pull it away. She'd never been self-conscious about her hands before. Callused and stained with varnish more often than not, they bore the marks of working with wood. Now, though, she wished they were smooth and soft and feminine. When he lifted her palm to his mouth, she flinched.

"Don't," he said, apparently guessing her thoughts. "Your hands are beautiful. Like the rest of you."

Her laugh had a forced sound to it. "You're not very observant," she said, finally giving in to the need to shield her hands from his gaze and clenching them together. "I know my hands are ugly."

He took both hands in his, turning the palms up. "I see hard work and pride in that work. That's nothing to be ashamed of."

There was no doubting the sincerity in his voice. Then why couldn't she accept it?

"You don't believe me."

"I do . . . it's just that I'm not used to . . ."

"Compliments?"

She nodded.

"Maybe you've been seeing the wrong men."

"Maybe I have." The truth was she

hadn't been seeing any men at all lately, at least not in the way he meant. Most men weren't interested in a woman who worked sixteen hours a day and smelled of sawdust. They wanted someone who was there for them at the end of the day, someone who wore satin and lace instead of denim and leather work boots.

Uncomfortable where they were heading, she checked her watch. "We ought to get back to work."

"Not yet. Lie down and relax."

To her surprise, she did just that, pillowing her head on her hands. When his hands began massaging the kinks from her neck and shoulders, she practically purred in pleasure. A breeze whispered over her, cooling her, inviting her to relax further.

"What's got you so tensed up?" he asked after long minutes had passed.

It was tempting to tell him of the headaches of trying to revitalize a business, to give in to the worry and fatigue of the last year. If she did, though, she feared she'd find it too comforting. She'd already told him far more about her past than most people knew. It didn't seem fair to burden him with the problems of the present as well.

Before she could give in to the need to confide in him any further, she shook off her drowsiness and pushed herself up. "Time to get back to work."

For a minute, she thought he was going to argue, but then he nodded.

The call had to be made. He'd put it off as long as possible. He punched in the long-distance number on a pay phone. "It's me."

"You took your time calling."

"I wanted to have something to report."

"What's she like?"

Grady took his time. "She's hard-working, talented, ambitious."

"Ambitious, you say?"

"She wants to make a success of her company," Grady said cautiously, wondering where Tyson was leading.

"Loans? Outstanding debts?"

"The bank holds the note on the loan she took out to buy equipment last year."

"What's her present situation?"

"She'd like to expand, hire more men," Grady said reluctantly.

"So she needs money." A satisfied note entered Tyson's voice. "Good."

"Why all the questions?"

"Nothing you have to worry about. Keep tabs on her. See what makes her tick."

"That's all?"

"For now. You got a problem with that?"

"I'd like to know where this is heading."

"You've been told what you need to know."

"What if I refuse?"

"Did I tell you I've talked with an old friend of mine in the Pentagon? Just a friendly chat. He served in 'Nam. Was over there about the same time as your brother. Maybe they even knew each other."

"I'll let you know when I've learned more."

Loyalty exacted a heavy price, Grady reflected as he hung up. A very heavy price. In a few words, Tyson had succeeded in reminding him of how he could destroy David with only a call.

Grady scowled at the phone. How much of his self could he sacrifice in an effort to protect his brother? More important, how could he live with himself after betraying Stephanie?

A self-loathing such as he'd never known before chilled him. He'd done Tyson's bidding before. None of those things had mattered — they were simply a question of straightening out trouble in the various factories and plants that Tyson owned.

Never had he been forced to involve himself with someone whom he could hurt.

He stepped up his work, whether to atone for his deception or to help meet the deadline, he wasn't sure. That night, he eased his sore body into bed. He hadn't lied when he told Stephanie he'd worked on construction sites all over the country, but that had been years ago. His muscles were paying the price for their unaccustomed workout during the last week.

The physical aches paled, though, compared to the torment his conscience was inflicting.

Chapter Four

"Grady, isn't it about time you came clean?" Stephanie asked as they'd finished for the day. After her revelations, she wanted — no, she needed — to know more about the man who'd come to mean so much to her in such a short time.

He stood motionless, his hand still on the piece of trimwork he had just finished sanding to a fine finish. "Come clean?"

"About why you're here."

"I'm here to work."

She looked at him in exasperation. "You're not an ordinary carpenter. Even if you're better with your hands than anyone I know, outside of my dad and Hank, you don't have the look."

"What do I look like?"

"Oh, maybe a private investigator." She entered into the guessing game with spirit, giving her imagination free rein. "Or a spy for the CIA."

Her words hit too close to home for comfort. "Nothing so glamorous, I'm afraid. I'm just a carpenter." His lips quirked into a wry smile. "Right now, an employed carpenter. And I've got a boss in a million." He cupped her chin in his hand. "For the first time in a long time, I like what I'm doing."

"I'm glad," she said simply.

That was a close one. He'd almost blown it with his fumbling words. The truth was bound to come out. The only choice he had was when.

Truth and honesty. Words he'd lived by. And now they were his enemy.

Stephanie sensed his discomfort with the subject and let it drop. They picked up their work, quickly reestablishing the easy rhythm between them. Only later did she remember that he hadn't answered her question.

Grady wiped eyes gritty with fatigue. Sleep had been a long time coming last night. Stephanie's question had rattled him more than he cared to admit. Whatever his inner turmoil, though, he couldn't let it interfere with his work.

Measuring a length of pine two-by-four, he thought of what he was creating here. A home.

Home.

It had been a long time since he'd used the word. Even longer since he'd had one.

He still didn't. Unless you counted the condominium that he treated more as a hotel room than a home. A cleaning woman came in twice a week and kept it free from dust and generally picked up. The stainless-steel refrigerator held little food, at most a wedge of cheese and a carton of milk, often stale. No, what he had wasn't a home. Four walls, the convenience of familiarity. But not a home.

Stephanie was making him want something that he'd forgotten the meaning of. The realization made him angry. He didn't need to be reminded of what might have been.

Grimly, he finished his measuring and cutting and nailed up the studs, taking out his frustration with every swing of the hammer. Gradually his anger slipped away to be replaced by determination. He needed to finish the framing. Legacies needed the bonus Mrs. Patterson promised if they finished ahead of schedule. Even more, *he* needed to do this for Stephanie.

Without talking, she held the stud in place. They worked quietly with a coordination that should have gratified him. Instead it emphasized what he was risking with his dishonesty.

"Grady, what's bothering you?"

Her voice startled him, but no more than her words. He'd thought he'd kept his worry to himself. Obviously, he wasn't as successful as he'd hoped. "What makes you think something's bothering me?" He kept his voice light.

"These," she said, tracing the lines around his mouth.

Gently, but deliberately, he eased away from her touch. "Hey, are we going to stand around talking or get this thing finished? Seems to me I remember something about a bonus."

He sensed her reluctance to drop the subject as she held one end of the cornice in place while he hammered a nail into it. He was especially proud of that piece of work. They'd done it together, patterning it after copies of the original.

"Someday, maybe you'll trust me enough to share whatever it is that's bothering you."

He almost blurted it out. *It's not you I don't trust. It's me.*

"I do trust you," he said quietly. "But some things aren't mine to share."

"I know you had a life before you came here. This thing you can't tell me . . . is it related to that?"

In this, at least, he could be honest. "Yes."

"Thank you."

"For what?"

"For not lying to me."

A wave of guilt washed over him at her words. "Stephanie . . ."

"Yes?"

He wanted to ask for her forgiveness. But to do so would require telling her everything. And that he was not prepared to do.

Not yet.

The rhythm of measuring, sawing, and nailing soothed his nerves, and he managed to push away his worry. For now. For now it was enough that he was with Stephanie. He caught himself pausing every once in a while, just to watch her. He didn't believe he'd ever grow tired of looking at her.

She always managed to look lovely, yet she paid little attention to her looks. It was one of the many facets of her personality that fascinated him. Right now, her lip was caught between her teeth as she frowned over the blueprints.

"Something wrong?" he asked.

She looked up. "Nothing that can't be fixed." She paused. "Did I button my shirt the wrong way?"

"What? Uh . . . no."

"Why are you staring?"

"Because you're beautiful."

He blew the bangs from her eyes, brushing a wisp of a kiss against her forehead.

A soft laugh escaped her. "When's the last time you had your eyes checked? I've got sawdust in my hair, dirt under my fingernails, and dirt on my face." She smoothed her hair back.

He took her hands and brought them to her sides. "Don't. And my eyes are just fine. You have fire in your hair, hands that show you know how to work, and the most kissable lips I've ever seen."

The denial hovering on her lips died at his last words. "Most kissable lips?"

"Definitely." He touched his lips to hers to prove his point.

"You're crazy."

"I know."

"I guess it's a good thing I'm sort of crazy too. Otherwise, I'd probably tell you to get lost."

"A very good thing," he agreed, kissing her once more and wondering if the day would come when she'd tell him just that.

A slow flush crept into her cheeks. She gave him a quick smile before bending her head over the sheaf of papers, her hair curtaining her face.

Grady smiled at her shyness, a pleasant contrast to most of the women he'd known. They accepted compliments as their due, while Stephanie seemed inordinately pleased with each one. His hands tightened around the hammer he was holding as he remembered that he had no right to give her compliments when he couldn't give her the most important thing of all — the truth.

Soon, he promised himself, he'd find a way to end the lies between them. Then he'd be free to give her everything she needed. Until then . . .

"Grady?"

"Hmm?"

"You were staring again."

"Sorry. I was thinking."

"You looked so troubled. Won't you let me help you?" She hesitated. "Is it money? If it is, maybe I could —"

"It's not money," he said, more harshly than he'd intended. Her quick generosity, given her circumstances, stunned him.

Her eyes clouded. "I didn't mean to offend you."

"You didn't. I just wasn't expecting . . . I know you're struggling . . ."

"If you're trying to say money's tight right now, you're right. But I could swing a few hundred dollars if it'd help."

"No one's ever done anything like that for me," he said, his voice husky. "But I really don't need money." He needed something much more precious. He needed her forgiveness. But he couldn't tell her that. Not now.

She gave him an uncertain look. "I know I'm not paying you what you could earn somewhere else. A man with your skills —"

"You're paying me plenty. Now, let's get back to work. Okay?"

"Okay."

He was careful to keep his worries to himself for the rest of the day. Stephanie didn't need any more on her plate than she already had. He only wished his problem *could* be solved with money.

Her warm heart would — should — compel a man, a better man, to keep his distance. It should, but it didn't. It drew him even as he told himself he should stay away.

She deserved better than a man who could only offer her lies.

When quitting time came, he kept working. If they completed the framing that day, they'd be able to start the

83

sheetrocking tomorrow. Though Stephanie hadn't said anything lately about meeting the deadline, he knew it was always there in the back of her mind.

"You some kind of glutton for punishment?" Hank asked.

The foreman had taken to stopping by the Patterson place after knocking off at the Conrad house. He'd said it was to touch base with Stephanie, but Grady knew differently. Hank didn't trust him. A humorless smile touched his lips as he conceded that the foreman had every right not to trust him.

"I'm almost finished."

"The boss can't afford to pay overtime."

"I wasn't asking for any." Grady kept his voice even. He knew the foreman didn't trust him. Under the circumstances, he didn't blame him.

Grady picked up another two-by-four and measured it, marking where he needed to saw it.

"You don't talk much, do you?" Hank observed.

"I always figured I'd learned more listening than talking."

"And keep yourself private from others."

Grady hunched a shoulder in acknowledgment. "There's that."

84

"Stephanie's got a lot riding on this job."

"I know."

"You're pretty handy with a saw," Hank allowed, the grudging note of admiration in his voice causing a smile to tug at Grady's lips.

The smile wasn't returned.

With a shrug, Grady turned back to his measuring. "I'm doing my job. Got a problem with that?"

"No," the foreman said slowly. "No problem. Just stick to your work and we'll get along fine." Still, he didn't leave. "She cares about you."

Grady had no answer for that. Hank had spoken no more than the truth.

"Don't hurt her."

"I don't intend to."

Hank gave him a long look. "I think you mean that. That doesn't mean she won't get hurt. I've known Stephanie since she was eleven. She doesn't give her heart easily. In fact, she's never even —"

Whatever he'd been about to say ended abruptly. It wasn't hard to figure out what he'd left unsaid, though. Stephanie was as innocent as a baby in the ways of love. Hank was right to be concerned about her.

"Forget I said anything," he said gruffly.

"She wouldn't take kindly to my inter-fering."

"No. I don't suppose she would."

"And I wouldn't take kindly to anybody hurting her." He leveled a steady gaze at Grady.

Message received, Grady telegraphed back. No words had been spoken; there was no need.

When Hank left, Grady let out a pent-up breath. He felt like he'd been walking a tightrope. Under other circumstances, he had a feeling he'd like the foreman. Heck, he *did* like him.

His shirt was plastered to his back, so he pulled it off. A slight breeze found its way through the roughed-in windows. He let the cool air trickle over him.

"Grady?" Stephanie's voice called up to him.

"Up here."

"What was Hank doing here?" she asked.

"Not much. Just giving me some ad-vice."

"Warning you off me?"

He hesitated before nodding briefly. "Yeah."

"He has no right," she began.

"He cares about you."

"You're right. Still, he shouldn't —"

"Leave it. No harm done."

She looked at him uncertainly. "You're sure?"

"Yeah. Hank's an all-right guy. He's just looking out for you."

"I know. He can't seem to get it through his head that I'm grown up."

"Well, I, for one, have no problem believing that at all." He raised his eyebrows in a suggestive leer that had her giggling.

"Now that we've established that I'm all grown up, why don't you tell me what you're doing here?"

"Just trying to keep my promise."

She didn't ask what promise. She already knew. The promise he'd given her that they'd finish on schedule. A man who kept his promises in this age of lost honor was rare indeed.

She didn't argue with him this time over the rightness of his unpaid overtime but laid a hand on his arm. "Thank you." Her glance rested briefly on the scars that bisected his chest.

The self-consciousness he'd felt when she'd first seen the scars had faded, but he still felt exposed and started to shrug on his shirt.

She laid a hand on his, stilling it. "Don't.

They don't bother me."

"No?"

Soft color shaded her cheeks as she admitted that the scars *did* bother her. But not in the way he meant. "Only because they mean you were hurt." Deliberately, she pressed a kiss to his shoulder.

The touch of her lips acted as balm to a pain long buried. The warmth of her breath on his neck stretched his nerves taut. His gaze collided with hers, and his heart beat a rapid tattoo against his chest at what he read in her eyes.

Wisps of hair escaped the clips to curl in damp tendrils along her temples. His fingers itched to brush them back from her face. With an effort, he kept his hands at his sides.

"Someday, maybe you'll trust me enough to tell me what happened." Her hands traced the path her lips had forged just moments earlier. "Until then, I can wait."

Her understanding should have warmed him. Instead, it filled him with self-revulsion.

Stephanie was making him feel things he hadn't felt in years. Things he thought long dead. Things he believed he'd buried in a jungle more than a dozen years ago.

She'd reached out to him and found things he hadn't known about himself. She was teaching him to care — to care about others, but mostly about himself. How long had it been since he honestly cared what happened to him?

Too long.

He'd acted as Tyson's right-hand man for so long that he'd forgotten how to be anything else. Well, all that was going to change. *Had* changed, he corrected.

Grady had his own code of ethics. He'd developed it over the years, a hard-won set of rules he lived by. If they didn't match those of others, they at least allowed him to keep his self-respect.

And that was his biggest fear. He was in danger of losing that respect. If he lost that, he'd have nothing to offer her.

Or himself.

Chapter Five

"What say we take off for a couple of hours?" Grady suggested after they knocked off the following evening. Returning to work following dinner had become a habit. Tonight, though, he was restless and needed to get away from the job. "Pack a picnic and head out."

She made a face. "I've got paperwork to catch up on."

"It can wait. I'd say we've earned a little R and R."

Suddenly she smiled. "I'd say you're right." Her smile died as she remembered her empty refrigerator.

"What's wrong?"

"I haven't had time to do any shopping. About all I've got for a picnic is a half a loaf of stale bread."

"Not to worry. You don't have to do a thing. I'll take care of everything."

An impish grin snuck across her lips. "It's the peanut butter and pickle sandwiches, isn't it? You don't trust me."

"I trust you plenty. It's your cooking I'm not so sure about."

He made his escape before she could punch his arm.

A half hour later, Grady rapped on her door. "Ready?"

At her nod, he gestured to his truck. "Your chariot awaits."

He drove quickly, competently, as he did everything, she thought. When he parked the truck under a grove of aspen, she gave a tiny sigh of pleasure.

"How did you know this was my favorite place?"

"You've been here before?"

"Yeah. My dad used to bring me after we'd finished up for the day."

"If you'd rather, we can go somewhere else."

"Not on my account."

He tossed her a blanket and carried a bulging sack to a level patch of ground. He pulled out a paper cloth, a bucket of take-out chicken and carton of coleslaw, a bottle of grape soda, and two plastic wineglasses.

He poured soda into a glass and handed it to her.

"I thought white wine went with poultry."

"Only if you're unimaginative. Today, we're breaking the rules." He poured himself a glass and downed it in one gulp.

"One of the few truly wonderful drinks still around." He wiped his mouth appreciatively.

He watched as Stephanie ate three pieces of chicken, a carton of coleslaw, and drank two glasses of soda.

"That was good," she said, sounding surprised.

"You've got a purple mustache."

She started to wipe the offending stain away.

"Let me." He dabbed at her mouth with his napkin, the casual gesture oddly intimate.

He couldn't keep from touching her hair, letting his fingers sift through it. It spilled over his hand, a living thing of gold and red that caught and held the dying sun. Fascinated, he watched as the colors shifted, first lightening then darkening as the fading light played over it.

"You have beautiful hair," he said, unable to free it from his grasp.

"I always wanted to have pale blond hair," she said, a slight frown knitting her brows.

He couldn't imagine anything more lovely than the fall of amber silk splashing over his hand. "Why?"

"In California it seemed everyone had

this beautiful blond hair. I always thought if I had hair like that, then maybe some family would want to take me home." She laughed lightly. "It didn't happen."

He heard the leftover pain of a little girl wanting to belong to someone.

"Hey," she said, apparently sensing his feelings. "It's all right. The Jamesons came along." A soft smile touched her lips. "When I asked them why they picked me, Dad said he liked red hair and freckles."

Grady let the comment pass. He'd never describe her hair as simply red. The infinite shades denied such a simple description. He traced the dusting of freckles on her nose. "I do too."

He watched as color suffused her face. She had no idea how beautiful she was. In her, he caught a glimpse of how Laura must have looked twenty years ago, before the disease had ravaged her body.

Thoughts of Laura were too close to his reason for being here. Deliberately, he forced them away. Time enough to deal with them later.

He picked up the corners of the cloth and tied them into a loose knot. He stashed the whole thing in the back of his truck. "Dishes are done."

Remembering the accounts she hoped to

go over before tomorrow, she checked her watch. "We'd better get back."

"Not yet. Tell me what puts that faraway look in your eyes sometimes."

"You don't miss much, do you?"

He shrugged. "Not much. But you're not getting off the hook that easily."

A quick laugh betrayed her nervousness.

"Hey," he said, taking her hand and squeezing it lightly. "You don't have to if it makes you that uncomfortable."

"It's not that."

"Then what?"

She was tempted to overlook the question and switch to a safer subject, but the sincerity and interest she read in his eyes invited confession.

Maybe talking about it would help. A deep breath steadied her. "Sometimes I played the 'what-if' game."

"The what?"

"What if my mother . . . my birth mother . . . had wanted me and hadn't given me up? What if I'd been adopted at birth instead of when I was ten? What if the couple who planned to adopt me went ahead with it . . ." She shrugged. "There are lots of what-ifs. I must have gone through them all when I was being shuffled from one foster home to another."

"That can be a dangerous game."

"You're right. But I couldn't help wondering *if* I had done something differently, *if* I had been different, then maybe . . ."

"Don't," he ordered. "You're not to blame for any of it. *It was not your fault,*" he said, accenting each word for emphasis.

"Intellectually, I know that. But I'm not so sure about the rest of me. I used to lie awake at night, wondering why no one wanted me."

He reached for her at the same moment she cried, "Why? Why didn't anyone want me enough to keep me?"

"Stephanie," he began softly, watching as first anguish and then embarrassment crossed her face. "Let it go, honey. Don't fight it anymore."

"I'm not —" She clutched his shirt as the sobs overtook her.

He stroked her back and waited for the storm to pass. When the sobs subsided into an occasional hiccup, he eased her away enough that he could look at her.

"I know it hurt. But you can't keep blaming yourself for something that wasn't your fault. You were a child. You had no say in what other people did."

"I kept thinking there must be something wrong with me. Otherwise, my birth mother would have kept me. And the other people . . . the ones who were going to adopt me . . ."

"Have you ever thought that maybe your biological mother gave you up because she wanted something better for you, something she couldn't give you?"

She'd never thought of it that way. Chewing her lip, she wondered if he could be right.

"You sound like you know what she was feeling."

He was treading on dangerous ground here and picked his words carefully. "It's not hard to imagine. A young, probably unwed woman, looking to give her child a better life. It happens."

"I know."

The pain that crept into her voice tore at his insides, and he longed to erase it from her life as though it had never happened. Yet then, he acknowledged, she wouldn't be the woman she was.

He yearned to wipe away the self-doubt he read in her eyes and then wondered at his reaction to her. More than a decade had passed since he'd worried about anyone other than his brother.

"You're right. I can't change the past. No one can."

Her shoulders straightened, and he sensed the fighting spirit beneath the fragile air. More than anything, he admired such strength.

"I just wish I could convince you to believe in yourself, to realize you are a beautiful woman, one who has more love to give than most of us ever dream of having."

"I want to," she said. "But I'm afraid of depending on you, of caring about you. Each time I love someone, something happens. I loved the first people who were going to adopt me and then they gave me back. Like I was some kind of damaged goods that didn't meet their standards. Each time I'd start to get close to someone in a foster home, I'd get moved. I loved my mom and dad. And they died."

"You don't have to be afraid with me. I'll never leave you." Gently, oh, so gently, Grady traced the delicate line of her jaw with his lips. They glided, stroked, and caressed with their feather-light touch. When he lowered his mouth to find her own, she responded instinctively, opening her lips to his.

The sweetness he found there was so incredible, it threatened to take his breath away. Never had a kiss been like this.

"That's right, sweetheart," he encouraged when she hesitantly wound her arms about his neck.

His mouth dipped lower to find the vulnerable hollow of her throat.

Stephanie felt his hands tremble as they held her. This strong man was trembling — and she had caused it. The knowledge filled her with wonder.

"We have all the time in the world." His words triggered the unwanted memory that he still faced his greatest hurdle — that of telling Stephanie the truth.

"All the time in the world," she repeated, her eyes shining with the promise of tomorrows filled with newfound joy.

The happiness reflected in her eyes was a double-edged sword. He had put that there; he could just as easily destroy it when she learned of his deceit. He was locked into a web of lies that seemed bent on keeping them apart.

Her fingers traced his scars through the fabric of his shirt. "Can you tell me about it?"

He shook his head. "Not now, honey. Like I said, it was a long time ago. I don't want to dredge up the past. Especially when I can't change it."

"Yet you want me to tell you about my past," she reminded him. "It works both ways."

He gave her a crooked grin. "I guess you're right." He looked at her keenly. "Are you sure you want to hear this? It's not very pretty."

She touched his cheek. "I'm sure."

"I was eighteen when I joined the Marines," he began. "Green and eager to save the world."

She took his hand in hers and squeezed it. A fine sheen of perspiration broke out across his forehead.

"What happened?"

"We were out on patrol one day. A little kid — he couldn't have been more than ten or eleven — ran toward our unit. He was carrying a grenade. I called out to my men not to fire, thinking it was a fake. But one of them panicked. He dropped the kid. Later, we found that the grenade was a live one, but it didn't make any difference. We'd killed a child. I think a little of me died that day."

He stared unseeingly at the wall. "That's the way war is. After Grenada, I was sent to another hot spot and then another. There's no black or white, only a million shades of gray that kept getting grayer by the year. I don't think I even knew what was right or wrong anymore. I just kept going, trying to make sense in a world that had lost all reason."

It was the utter defeat in his tone that moved her most. Stephanie willed the tears, still clinging to her lashes, not to fall. Grady didn't want her sympathy. He'd be uncomfortable and embarrassed if he ever got a glimpse of it. She averted her face, knowing her feelings were reflected in her eyes.

He caught the slight movement. With gentle fingers, he captured her chin and forced her to face him. She attempted to brush the wetness away from her lashes, but he stilled her hand.

"Don't." He raised his hand and, with his knuckles, skimmed away the tears that had spilled over onto her cheeks.

"I'm not crying."

"I can see that." The gentle humor in his voice was almost her undoing.

"I'm not," she insisted.

"It's all right. Don't be ashamed of your tears. They're honest." He looked at her curiously. "Are they for me?"

Miserably, she nodded.

"No one's ever cried for me before." His voice turned husky. "I never wanted them to." He paused. "Until now."

She looked up, not sure she'd heard correctly. "You're not angry?"

"With you? Never."

The sincerity in his voice convinced her that he meant what he said. A sweet warmth stole through her as the significance of that dawned on her. A week ago, even a few days ago, he'd have withdrawn into himself if she'd breached the invisible boundaries that had so far defined their relationship. Now he accepted her tears and the caring that had prompted them.

She took his hand in hers, wanting to erase the loneliness that had been his sole companion for too many years. Tears now streamed down her cheeks unchecked.

He dabbed at them with his handkerchief. "It's over now. I survived. Even when I didn't want to. I must have been born under a lucky star."

She pressed his hand to her lips, wanting to absorb his pain and knowing she couldn't. "Tell me the rest."

"You're sure you want to hear?"

"Yes."

He kissed her before continuing. "From then on, I didn't much care what happened. It made me take risks no sane man would." A shutter dropped over his eyes as scene after scene unfolded in his mind. Unconsciously, he rubbed his left side, where a piece of shrapnel had embedded itself. He had dug it out with his own knife sterilized over an open fire.

Stephanie remained silent, waiting for the horror he was reliving to pass.

"I was promoted, then sent back to the States." He gave a short laugh. "I got a Purple Heart and was a two-minute hero. It took me two years to discover there were no jobs for vets." A half smile edged his lips. "Especially ones with my particular skills."

"What did you do?" she whispered.

"I bummed around, taking any job I could. When I was in LA, I met —" He paused. "— someone from my old outfit. He offered me a job."

"And your family?"

"My parents died a long time ago." Again, the faraway look masked his eyes. "It's been just David and I for a long time now."

"You're close?"

"Yeah. You could say that." He coughed to cover the huskiness that had crept into his voice. "David's eleven years older than me. He sort of looked out for me when we were growing up."

She tried to read between the lines. "What's he like?"

"David's an idealist. Not like me."

She let that pass. "Where is he now?"

"California. In a VA hospital at the moment. He has to go in every six months. I see him whenever I can."

"You love him very much."

He didn't answer that. "Look, what say we leave all this stuff where it belongs — in the past?"

Could their love override the scars of the past? Could she erase the loneliness that was so much a part of him and make him believe in a forever kind of love, the kind her parents had shared for over thirty-five years? She was honest enough to admit that nothing less would do for her.

A smile flashed through the horror his words had conjured up. Whatever time they had she would treasure. It would be enough. It had to be.

Saturday morning she hoped they might have a repeat of the picnic they'd shared a few days ago. When she saw Grady with a duffel bag heading to the trailer, she knew her hope wasn't to be realized.

She'd known a man like Grady wouldn't stick around a small-potatoes outfit like Legacies forever.

With what she prayed was a normal smile, she asked, "Going somewhere?"

"I've got to go out of town for a couple of days. Don't worry. I'll be here bright and early Monday morning."

"I wasn't . . ." The lie died on her lips. "I'm glad," she said instead.

He brushed his lips over hers. "Stephanie, I think you know how I feel. I want —"

She put a finger to his lips. "Don't, Grady," she whispered.

"Is it me?"

"No, it's me. I'm not ready. Not yet."

She needed time to adjust to the new things she was discovering about herself and about him. She wanted what her parents had had. Someone to share the ups and downs of life. Someone to rejoice with her and to cry with her. Someone who could make her feel loved and cherished. Someone she could count on.

She wasn't ready to put what she felt for him into words, or to hear those same words from him. Maybe someday. Maybe someday very soon.

Chapter Six

The Tyson mansion had never bothered him before. But now it loomed menacingly against the backdrop of mountain and sky, its stone turrets a tawdry imitation of the stately redwoods surrounding it.

Grady shielded his eyes against the glare of the late-afternoon sun that silhouetted the crests of the foothills with fiery crimson.

An unseasonable heat mingled with his own tense state had dampened his clothes with sweat. Impatiently, he tugged the tie free and undid the top button of his shirt.

He didn't look forward to the upcoming meeting. He'd worked for Trevor Tyson for over a decade, and, for the most part, they'd been good years. Now he was leaving. His sense of honor demanded he confront the colonel in person to tell him he was resigning. And why.

He hadn't called for an appointment. Surprise still served well when approaching the enemy. Military tactics die hard, he thought wryly.

After being announced and kept waiting

for thirty minutes, Grady acknowledged that he'd been outmaneuvered. When Trevor Tyson marched into the room, Grady stood.

"My aide said you wanted to see me," Tyson said. Even with his once ramrod-straight back slightly stooped, he was still every inch the colonel.

Grady watched as Tyson lowered his bulk into the leather chair behind the desk, folding his arms across his chest.

"Well, what do you want? I don't have all day." His mouth thinned to an uncompromising slit, Tyson tapped a pipe against the edge of the desk, glaring at the younger man.

"You never wanted Laura to find her daughter, did you?" The question wasn't one he'd planned to ask. He'd intended to resign and then leave.

Tyson templed his fingers, his hands resting on his chest. "No."

Even though he'd expected it, Tyson's answer still shook Grady. "Then why go to all the trouble to have me find Stephanie?"

"I like to know who I'm dealing with."

That rang true. Tyson was known as one of the toughest colonels in the Marines. Part of his reputation came by his insistence upon knowing the enemy. The tactic had earned him numerous victories in the field.

"What are you going to tell Laura?"

"Nothing."

"Maybe I'll tell her."

"Go ahead, if you want to see her hurt."

"How could finding her daughter hurt her?"

"Laura isn't strong. She doesn't need some freeloader coming around and sponging off her."

"Stephanie Jameson's no freeloader."

"Sure, sure. Didn't you say she was trying to get her business off the ground?"

"Yeah, but —"

"So it stands to reason that she's hard up for money. She's got a bank loan to pay off, right?"

"You're going to bribe her to stay away from Laura? Why tell her anything at all? Why not leave her alone?"

"Sooner or later, she's going to start looking for her mother. Laura's already registered with an agency that matches birth parents with adopted children. It's only a matter of time before they connect if the Jameson woman gets it in her head to do the same thing." Tyson shrugged. "I'm just buying some insurance."

"Insurance?"

"To make sure she doesn't go looking. If I pay her off, I'll have leverage if she tries to double-cross me and contact Laura."

Grady's lips tightened at the notion that Stephanie could be bought. "What about Laura?"

"If I tell Laura we tried and didn't find anything, she'll give up."

"You sure about that?"

Tyson looked annoyed. "Laura's my sister. She's always allowed herself to be guided by me."

"She could surprise you this time."

"Why don't you mind your own business and allow me to take care of my sister?"

Grady heard the warning and backed off. For now. He had no intention, though, of keeping Laura from the daughter she'd waited twenty-eight years to see.

"You're wrong if you think you can buy Stephanie off."

"Money talks."

Tyson's answer to everything — money.

"What are you so afraid of?" Grady asked.

The colonel drew himself up. "You just keep an eye on her. Let me know if her financial situation changes significantly. I'll take care of the rest."

"You're wrong about Stephanie."

Tyson grinned. "Never knew you to go overboard about some woman. What's the matter? Going soft in your old age?"

What's the matter is working for you. But Grady didn't say the words aloud. He knew Tyson was a tough businessman and a fierce competitor, whether on the battle-field or off, but never before had he realized the extent of the man's ruthlessness.

Tyson was preparing to betray his own sister without so much as a thought to her feelings.

"I want out."

"Out?" The colonel looked at him as though examining a bug under a micro-scope. "Why?"

"I've been working for you for over ten years. It's time I got on with my life."

Tyson eyed Grady shrewdly. "You never complained before."

"Never had reason to." He lifted a shoulder. "Things change."

"You're thinking of finding a different job?"

"Maybe."

"You're losing your edge."

"No. It's taken me a while, maybe too long, but I'm just beginning to find it."

Tyson inspected Grady with new in-terest. "Why don't you tell me about it?"

When Grady hesitated, the colonel added, "We've been friends for a lot of years."

That was not how Grady would describe their relationship. "It's time I thought about settling down."

"Settling down? Have you got someone in mind?"

"I'm in love with Stephanie." He was startled at hearing himself say the words aloud. He hadn't meant to blurt it out like that. Instinctively, he knew he'd made a tactical error. Still, he savored the taste of the words upon his lips, knowing they were the most important he would ever say.

Tyson appeared unmoved. "So?"

"So, I can't continue working for you," Grady explained, eyeing the colonel warily. He knew Tyson wasn't feebleminded. Apparently, he was being obtuse for reasons of his own.

"As soon as you've brought me what I want," Tyson said, "you're free to do whatever you want. If you want the woman, you're welcome to her. It's nothing to me either way. Though I'd hate to see you throw away your life on a little nobody like her."

"That little nobody is your niece."

"A matter of chance. She'll never be a Tyson."

"Maybe she doesn't want to be."

The colonel snorted. "Look around you. Can you honestly tell me that she wouldn't want a part of all this?"

Grady let his gaze wander around the opulent room, the carefully chosen antiques, the priceless Persian rug, and wondered about Stephanie's reaction. She'd undoubtedly appreciate their beauty, but the price tag of such things would never impress her.

"Yes."

"Then you're as crazy as my sister. She's willing to hand it all over, everything I've worked to build for her, to someone she hasn't set eyes on in twenty-eight years."

"What she wants to do with her own money is her choice."

"Laura owns fifty percent of Tyson Enterprises. Do you think I'd let her give it all away to some little upstart?"

So that was it.

"I'm through," Grady said, stressing each syllable and ignoring the reference to Stephanie.

The colonel didn't appear upset. He examined his fingernails. "I hate to lose you, Grady, but . . ." A look of regret crossed his face. "I guess your loyalty is just so much lip service, isn't it?"

"Loyalty?"

"You told me you'd do anything to protect David. But now you're letting a woman come between you and your brother."

Grady gripped the desk in front of him. Tyson was a master of manipulation. He knew just what buttons to push, when to apply the pressure, and when to back off.

Grady thought of David and how the colonel could destroy the fragile peace he'd managed to achieve. The next moment Stephanie's face, her eyes shining with trust, flashed before his face. Whatever happened with David, they'd work it out together. He turned to leave.

Tyson's next words halted him. "I suppose you won't mind if I tell my niece you've been working for me."

Grady forced himself to keep his voice casual even as a chill sprinted down his spine. "What do you mean?" Deliberately, he kept his back to the colonel, wanting time to compose himself. He'd erred badly by giving away too much already.

"I think she's entitled to hear the truth. That you tracked her down, wormed your way into her confidence, and then betrayed her." Tyson's voice rang with self-righteousness and something more. Triumph?

It wasn't the truth, but it was close enough. Acknowledging the inevitable, Grady turned slowly. "What do you want?" He thrust aside the urge to close his hands around the man's throat and met the colonel's gaze. Cold. Never had he seen such cold eyes. Why had he never noticed before the emptiness in Tyson's eyes?

"I want to make sure she never bothers my sister."

Grady remained impassive under Tyson's inspection, his emotions once more in check.

The colonel looked at Grady shrewdly.

Grady regretted his earlier anger. It wouldn't help Stephanie, and it fired Tyson's temper.

"You don't want me for an enemy, Chapman."

Grady recoiled from a cold so intense that it touched his very core.

He stood. "You're sick. There's no way I'll let you get away with hurting Stephanie."

"Don't start spouting your petty morality to me," Tyson said. "It's a little late for that, don't you think? You'll do whatever it takes to get the job done. Just like you've always done."

"What do you mean?"

"Exactly what I said. You've played hardball in the past. So don't give me this nonsense about how you've changed. I don't buy it. And, if you're honest, you don't either. You know, you and I are a lot alike. That's why we've gotten along so well over the years."

Nauseated at the possibility that Tyson was right, Grady stared at him. He shook his head as though to deny it.

"You don't want to believe it, do you?"

"You're wrong about me."

Tyson snorted. "If I am, it's your loss. You lose your edge in this business, and you're out. You of all people ought to know that." He eyed his opponent slyly. "What about Stephanie? What if I tell her you went there with the sole purpose of spying on her?"

Grady took a menacing step forward.

"I can have five men here before you take another step," Tyson told him. He held a finger poised over a button built into his desk. "But you still want to strangle me, don't you?"

Grady's growl was answer enough.

"Interesting," the colonel mused. "In all the years I've known you, I've never seen you lose your temper. Now, within the space of a few minutes, you lose it twice."

When Grady remained silent, he said, "We've always gotten along well. But now you've fallen under her spell. You can't even think straight."

With a visible effort, Grady checked his anger yet again. He would get nowhere this way. He swallowed hard. "Why would you tell Stephanie I work for you?" he asked reasonably. "You'd be cutting off your only source of information to her."

"I won't have to tell her," Tyson said, "*if* you do as you're told." He smiled affably and patted Grady's shoulder. "Let's have no more talk like that. We've always had a good working relationship. I'd hate to see anything interfere with that. Especially some bimbo."

Grady deliberately shrugged off Tyson's hand, not bothering to hide the distaste he felt at the other man's touch. He knew enough about his boss to know that Tyson wouldn't be dissuaded from his goal. His only hope was to pretend to stick with the job and find a way to help Laura and Stephanie while protecting David at the same time.

"I'll do what it takes," he said and started to leave. At the door, he paused. His gaze pinned Tyson's and held it. "Don't ever tell me again we're alike. You and I have nothing in common."

He turned and walked away. This time he didn't look back.

Grady couldn't get away from the house and its owner fast enough. He felt like he was suffocating. He drove quickly, almost recklessly, stopping only when he came to a lookout point. He parked the car and got out. His gaze spanned the breathtaking vista before him, no less spectacular in the evening dusk. Vivid pinks, rich purples, and all the shades in between vied with one another to create a sunset of intense beauty.

Greedily, he drank in great gulps of fresh air. Even the state-of-the-art air-conditioning system that regulated the temperature in Tyson's mansion couldn't wash away the oppressive air that hung over the house like a death shroud.

He stretched as though to free himself of invisible manacles. For too long, he'd allowed habit to chain him to a man who used and then discarded people. Not that he'd been blind to Tyson's faults, but he'd accepted them as part of the package. Now his loyalty to such a man sickened him. He shuddered at the thought that, if he stayed, he might succumb to the forces that drove Tyson, losing his humanity and compassion in a quest for power.

He had lied to Tyson.

And he would do it again if he had to. He had told Tyson he'd do the job, but there was no way he was going to betray Stephanie now. She meant too much to him. She was life and breath to him. Without her, he would have no reason for being.

He had to buy time.

Every second with her, every minute, was one more opportunity to forge the bonds between them. One more bit of armor against the pain to come.

Grady drove quickly, as anxious to put as many miles between Tyson and himself as he was to return to Stephanie.

In his mind, he replayed the conversation until each word was burned into his memory. Tyson was right about one thing: if Stephanie learned from him how Grady had insinuated himself into her life, she would hate him.

The only solution was for him to tell her the truth himself. He had known it all along. Yet he desperately searched for some other way, even knowing as he did so that it was hopeless.

With Stephanie, there could be no halfway measures. He was in love with her.

Not infatuated, though he almost wished it were so. He could have dealt with that. Love had a different flavor; it couldn't be rushed, and it wasn't greedy. Love demanded freedom to grow. Love was a seed that must be nourished, nurtured as it unfolded, cherished as it blossomed into full bloom. Love was forever.

And he was scared.

By driving all day, he reached the outskirts of Colorado Springs just after midnight. He knocked lightly on her trailer door. The need to see her kept him on the step even when good manners dictated he leave.

Just when he would have turned away, a light switched on.

"Grady?"

"Yes."

The door swung open, and she all but threw herself into his arms.

"I was hoping you'd make it back tonight," she said, pulling her robe more tightly about her.

Grady grinned as he slipped his arms around her waist. "I was enjoying the view," he teased. "Miss me?" His fingers sketched tiny patterns down her spine, nearly wiping away rational thought.

"Yes." No games between them. What they had was too important.

"I like to hear you say it."

"I missed you," she said, her voice whisper-soft.

"That's all I needed." He led her by the hand to sit with him on the sagging sofa.

"I feel like you've been away forever," she confessed as he kissed her.

"It seems like I have.

"That feels so good," she murmured as he held her close, her words muffled against his chest. "I don't want you to ever stop holding me."

"There's so much I want to share with you." He stopped to turn her face to his, cupping her chin in his hand. "Do you know what I'm saying?"

"I think so."

"You make me want things I haven't dared let myself think about in years. You make me hungry for something I didn't think existed any more. You make me feel when I thought all feeling was dead. I can't imagine my life without you in it."

Stephanie was startled. It was a long speech for a man not given to fancy words.

Tears puddled in the corners of her eyes as she held him close. In many ways, she'd had a rough life, yet it didn't compare with the barren existence Grady painted for her. She cried silently for the lonely man she cradled in her arms.

I'm here for you, she wanted to say. Instead, she curled her arms around him and held him tighter.

For a fragment of a moment, they stayed there, locked together, their breath mingling.

A feeling of peace settled over him. The self-disgust he felt for the lie he was living wasn't enough to move him out of her embrace.

He felt he could stay this way forever, with Stephanie's arms wrapped around him. He needed this, now more than ever. Now that he'd discovered just how far he was willing to go to protect her.

Never had anything felt so good — so right — as this sweet communion of spirit he felt with Stephanie. With every bit of willpower he possessed, he freed himself, and looked at the woman who'd turned his life upside down in a few short weeks.

Tell her the truth, his conscience prodded. *Better coming from you than from Tyson.* Still, he hesitated. *Tell her,* the voice persisted. *Tell her who you are and why you came here. If you do it now, there's a chance she won't throw you out.*

Sure, the other, cowardly side of himself argued. *Tell her you came here to spy on her and then report back to the man who convinced your mother to give you up in the first place. She'll love that.*

"Stephanie, I have —"

She skimmed a finger along his lips. "Not now. Don't say anything. It's enough that you're here." She reached up to frame his face in her hands. "I know there's something bothering you. I also know you'll tell me when the time is right. Until then . . ." A smile brushed her lips. "I can wait."

Her simple trust in him shamed him even as it humbled him. He didn't deserve it . . . or her. But he was going to change all that. With only a few words, he could wipe away the lies that stood between them. He could also shatter that very fragile bond linking them.

Maybe it was a good thing she'd stopped his confession.

It gave him what he needed most — time. Every second with her, every minute, was one more fraction of time of faith-building between them. One more bit of armor against the pain he knew would come. One more thread of hope that when it was over, she might find it in her to forgive him.

"I never want to hurt you." He realized

he'd spoken the words aloud.

"I know."

Her simple faith warmed him. She was so trusting, so honest, that she couldn't conceive of anyone being otherwise.

Silently, he prayed he could keep the promise he'd just made.

"*I* have something to tell *you*," she said.

"Confession time?"

"Sort of."

"Sounds pretty serious."

"It is." She took a deep breath. "I'm afraid if you stay much longer I won't be able to let you go. And that's not fair to you. I don't think I could bear it if you leave. . . ."

"I'm not leaving," he promised. "Not unless you ask me to."

"That's not going to happen."

"I hope you're right."

She frowned. "I don't understand —"

"It's nothing," he said, tunneling his hand beneath her hair. "Nothing important."

She melted against him. "I'm glad you're back."

"You said that already."

"So I did. Must be because I missed you so much."

She pulled his hand to her lips and softly kissed his palm.

He replaced his hand with his lips.

The kiss was a dream come true. Her eyes closed, she memorized this moment . . . the heat of his lips, the rasp of his beard against her cheeks, the sounds of the night.

"I didn't know it could be this way," she said when he raised his head, awe in her voice.

Her simple admission filled him with wonder while at the same time humbling him.

Shyly, she put her arms around his neck, bringing his face at a level with hers. She touched her lips to his. He reeled under her power though her touch was as light as thistledown.

She rained tiny kisses along his throat, each a sweet promise for the future. His control, which he'd always prided himself upon, was now threatened by a touch so soft it barely registered yet so potent that it honed his senses to a fine pitch.

"Stephanie," he whispered, "you make me feel things I shouldn't be feeling."

I know, she responded silently, feeling the sweet ache of desire and knowing she wanted him as she had no other man. For an instant, she allowed herself to indulge in a fantasy: she and Grady married, with the promise of children to come. She'd always wanted a big family.

His heart spoke to hers; hers answered in return. Silently, he was telling her what she longed to hear. She rested against him, content to draw from his quiet strength.

His chin rested on her head. He fingered the curls framing her face and inhaled the fresh scent that clung to her hair.

"I can't keep on this way," he said, his voice hoarse with repressed longing. "I can't keep working for you and pretend I feel nothing when the other men are around."

She didn't say anything but waited.

"I think you know how I feel. I want to be part of your life."

She murmured an inarticulate sound.

"If I'm off track, let me know. But I need to hear it from you."

"You're not off track," she managed to say. "But I'm not ready —"

He stopped her. "I know that. I don't want to rush you. But I'm not a patient man. I need to know what you're feeling."

"I couldn't ask you — or any man — to share the debts I've accumulated."

"What if he wanted to?"

Tears stung her eyes at his words.

"I understand pride. But it doesn't belong between two people who . . ."

He didn't finish the sentence, and for that she was grateful.

"I know you're afraid of caring . . . of loving." There, he'd said it. "Don't let the past come between us. It can't hurt you anymore. Not unless *you* let it. Let it go."

"I don't know if I can." Her eyes begged him to understand. "I want to. More than you know, I want to."

He brushed the back of his hand against her cheek. "That's enough. All I wanted to know was that I wasn't imagining what was happening between us."

"You weren't."

"If you ever want me to go away, you'll have to tell me. Because nothing else could make me leave you."

Warm hands cupped her face as he searched for an answer there.

She put a tentative hand to his cheek, touched by his declaration but still afraid to trust her own feelings. "Grady, you . . . me . . . how can you know for sure?"

"Because it's as much of a part of me as breathing. *You're* a part of me." He gathered her to him, cradling her in his arms. Still, he couldn't get enough of her. He felt her heartbeat race, matching the rhythm of his own.

"Grady, I need time," she said when he released her.

"I know. I didn't mean to rush you. It's been so hard trying to keep my feelings to myself. I just needed to know that what we feel for each other is real."

"It's real," she whispered. "More real than anything has ever been before."

"That's all I needed to know. We'll work everything else out. Together." *We have to*, he added silently.

Grady liked to think he had too much integrity to give promises he didn't believe he could keep. He'd promised Stephanie that they'd meet the deadline on the Patterson job. Simple. All that required was hours of hard work and skill.

He'd also promised not to leave her unless she asked him to. Again, simple. Nothing would tear him away from her unless she told him to leave. He'd given one more promise — to love her for the rest of his life. He wouldn't have any problem fulfilling that.

He knew Stephanie was wary of caring too deeply. *"Everyone I've ever loved has left me,"* she'd said.

It was up to him to convince her that love was a promise they could keep together.

Chapter Seven

His work took on a new energy. He wasn't worried at meeting the schedule — he knew they'd make the deadline. No, that wasn't what was driving him. It was Stephanie and the happiness he saw in her eyes. He'd do anything to keep it there.

Other events seemed to be spiraling out of his power, but work was something he could control. He caught her gaze resting on him curiously when he worked through their break.

He looked at her down-bent head, her hair catching the light and turning to gold. As if aware of his scrutiny, she raised her head just then, her eyes meeting his, her lips curving softly into a smile.

Yeah. He'd do anything to make her happy. Anything but tell her the truth. Suddenly the arguments he'd used last night to justify his delay fell flat. Time wouldn't change the fact that he'd lied to her. Nothing could change that.

He stole a glance at her. He couldn't tell her. Not now. Not when her eyes were filled with happiness. Not when they looked at him with such trust. Not when all he wanted to do was take her into his arms and promise to love her forever.

Coward.

Yeah.

"What do you say we break for lunch?" she asked. "It's almost noon."

"Sounds good."

They ate their sandwiches with only the barest conversation between them. When he tossed the rest of his lunch in the trash and picked up the power sander, Grady knew she was puzzled, but he was powerless to explain why he'd worked like a man possessed.

She lifted her lips. "Kiss me. Please."

He couldn't erase the questions from her eyes. But he could kiss the lips she offered to his. He could give her — give them both — this moment. He could, and he would.

He bent his head and tasted heaven.

"Stephanie, my sweet Stephanie, I think I've loved you forever. I've loved you and didn't even know you. I've been waiting for you. Only for you."

She looked up at him, shaken by the emotion in his voice, the pain she read in his face.

"Whatever happens, remember that I

love you." He gripped her shoulders. "Promise."

She looked at his eyes, stricken now with fear rather than pain. "You're frightening me."

He released his grip and brushed his hands over her hair. "I'm sorry. That's the last thing I want to do."

"Tell me, Grady. Whatever it is, we'll face it together. There's nothing you can't say to me."

"I wish it were that simple."

A shiver raced down her spine. His fear was contagious.

He drew her to him. "I love you. You have to believe that. No matter what happens, remember that I love you." He took her face between his hands. "Will you do that for me?"

"I'll remember," she said softly, still not understanding his urgency but frightened anyway.

"Promise," he ordered roughly. "You've got to promise."

Surprised by his intensity, she nodded. "I promise." She rubbed her cheek against his work-callused· palm and relaxed when his grip on her gentled.

"I'm sorry. I didn't mean to hurt you." Tenderly he stroked the nape of her neck with his thumb, unerringly finding its sensitive base.

"You didn't." She twisted in his arms so that his lips now rested on the curve of her shoulder.

"I don't deserve you."

"Don't say that. Don't ever say that." She held him tightly, as though she could ward off the demons chasing him. Whatever they were, she and Grady would fight them. Together.

At last, he lifted his head. His eyes were bleak, but his lips had curved into the smile she was beginning to recognize. "You're one special woman, Stephanie. But you know that already, don't you?"

She continued to hold him. Whatever was troubling him couldn't defeat them as long as they were together. She had to believe that.

"How'd I get so lucky?" Grady murmured.

"I'm the lucky one," she said, and knew it was true.

"Stephanie Jameson?"

A slightly stooped man with graying hair stood in her doorway. A banker type, she decided, panic coiling in her stomach. She didn't recognize him from the local

130

branch, but he could be a loan officer from the main office.

A dozen scenarios flashed through her mind, each more awful than the next. Her note. He'd come to collect . . . Her mind rejected that. Her payments were current.

"Trevor Tyson."

Carefully wiping her hands on her jeans, she held out her hand. "Mr. Tyson. What can I do for you?"

"It's more like what I can do for you."

"I don't understand —" Her words died as he handed her a check. She scanned it, her eyes widening at the amount. "Why?"

She hadn't believed in Santa Claus for a long time, but a check like this might have her changing her mind. Even as she allowed herself a moment's fantasy of what she could do with the money, she was handing it back. "I don't know who you are, but no one gives this kind of money away for nothing. So I'm asking again. Why?"

He ran a hand through his iron-gray hair. A muscle twitched in his cheek. But it was his eyes she focused on. Gray like his hair, they were as cold as the wind that whipped down from the Colorado Rockies in January.

"The money's to leave my sister alone."

"Your sister?" What did his sister have to do with her? Maybe the man was truly insane. She took an instinctive step back.

"Don't play innocent with me, Ms. Jameson."

"I don't have time to play games. So why don't you tell me why you're here?" She resisted the urge to squirm under the scrutiny he subjected her to. Who was this man and what did he want with her?

"You favor her," he said at last. "Around the eyes."

"Who?"

"You really don't know, do you?"

"Know what?"

On anyone else, the twist of his lips might have been a smile, but the twisting of his lips had her stepping back once more, seeking to widen the space between them.

"Laura would have found you eventually," he said.

She had the impression he wasn't talking to her but to himself, trying to come to grips with something.

"Laura?"

"Your mother. My sister."

"My mother died . . ." His words finally took on meaning. "My mother wants to see me?" Hope, anger, and fear fused together.

"She thinks she does. That's why I'm giving you this." He thrust the check back in her hands. "Stay away from her. She doesn't need you messing up her life."

This time, with a calm she didn't feel, she tore the check in pieces. "Keep your money, Mr. Tyson. I don't need it."

He looked around, contempt in his gaze as he took in her cramped quarters. "No?"

The faint sneer in his voice had her lifting her chin, but she held her temper. "No. If I decide I want to see my mother, no amount of money could keep me away." She asked the question uppermost on her mind. "How did you find me?"

"I wondered when you'd get around to asking that. It wasn't hard. All it took was money."

"You'd know all about that."

He nodded complacently. "I've known where you were for some time now. I've just been waiting for the right time." He inspected his well-manicured hands.

"Right time for what?"

"The right time to make my offer. I heard you were thinking about expanding and thought you might need capital. The kind that doesn't need to be repaid."

"What makes you think I'd take your money?"

"You have a substantial bank note to pay back. Your foreman is thinking of leaving to find a better-paying job. Your equipment is outdated, your crew understaffed."

How had he learned so much about her?

He must have seen the question in her eyes, for he smiled. "It pays to hire the best. I like to think I get what I pay for."

"The best?"

"I believe you have a new man working for you?"

She nodded. Grady. The best thing that ever happened to her. Her breath jammed in her throat as his implication sank in. Tyson couldn't mean Grady.

"Chapman always delivers the goods."

Not Grady. It couldn't be Grady! her heart screamed. *Please, don't let it be Grady.* She must have given voice to her prayers, for Tyson nodded.

"That's right. Grady Chapman. He's worked for me for . . . oh, let's see, over ten years now. He served under me in the Marines."

He read the shock in her eyes and smiled, a cold travesty of a smile. "What's the matter? Did he fail to mention he worked for me? Don't feel bad. It must have slipped his mind."

At last she found her voice. And her

134

faith. "I don't believe you."

"Of course you don't. Why don't we wait? I'm sure he'll be happy to tell you all about it."

She held onto her belief that he was lying. Somehow he'd found out Grady was working for her and was now trying to implicate him. She didn't know this man standing before her, but she felt his coldness, saw the loathing in his eyes.

What she didn't understand was why.

She'd never met him before. Why did he hate her? If his sister were her mother, that would make him her uncle. Why was he so anxious to keep them apart? She wasn't aware of asking the question aloud until she saw his hands clench around the cane. She took an instinctive step backward at the hate that spilled from his eyes.

"Laura's worth millions."

Understanding came slowly and, with it, rage. "And you think I want part of it?"

The rasping sound coming from her throat startled her until she identified it as laughter. But the laughter had no mirth in it. It was as cold as the eyes of the man who glared at her.

"Don't pull that goody-two-shoes act with me. Everyone wants more. Especially a little nobody like you who's out for everything she can get. You think I don't know how you got those suckers who took you in to leave you everything they had."

For a moment she thought of the debts her father had left her. She didn't intend to share that with Tyson, though. "My parents left me the most important thing of all. Love."

"Love?" He snapped his fingers. "That's all it's worth."

She saw him then for what he was — a pathetic old man who would never know the joy of loving and being loved.

The idea that this man with such a twisted mind might be related to her filled her with revulsion. If his sister was anything like him . . . Stephanie shook her head. He'd told her that Laura was looking for her. Laura couldn't be like her brother.

"My *parents* . . ." Stephanie stressed the word. ". . . gave me a home and love. That's all I ever wanted from them."

His hoarse laugh disintegrated into a cough. A series of spasms shuddered through him.

Instinctively, she stepped forward to steady him, but he shrugged off her hand with a snarl.

She looked at him more carefully and noticed the telltale signs of age that she'd missed before. The iron-gray hair showed traces of white; his shoulders were stooped. The hand gripping the silver cane quivered ever so slightly. But if his body showed signs of weakness, his eyes didn't. Cold and gray, they pierced through her, causing a shiver to skate down her spine.

Unconsciously, she straightened her shoulders. "We have nothing to say to each other. You can leave anytime."

He surveyed her with surprise, perhaps even admiration. "You've got a lot to say for yourself. I like that."

She doubted that. She doubted he liked anything — or anyone — who dared to defy him.

"I'll wait. I've got some business to finish up with Grady."

The arrogance of the man was unbelievable. She was about to throw him out when the door to the trailer opened.

"Stephanie." Grady took in her ashen face and dropped the bag of nails he was holding. A premonition settled over him even as he asked, "What happened?"

"I don't know. Maybe you can tell me." Her voice was even, her face expressionless.

He took a hard look at her. It had happened. Still, he hoped he was wrong. "I have to —"

"What's the matter, Chapman?" Tyson interrupted, stepping into view. "Haven't told her the truth yet?" He glanced from one to the other, clearly enjoying himself.

"Truth?" she repeated dully. She looked at the man who meant more to her than life itself. *Tell me he's lying,* she begged him silently.

"Chapman's one of my best men," her uncle told her, satisfaction evident in his smirk. "I sent him to find you, and find you he did."

Stephanie stared at Grady, willing him to deny it. Her eyes implored him to tell her it wasn't true, that it was all some horrible mistake. He stretched out a hand to her before letting it drop.

"I know I should have told you sooner. I tried. I really tried. I just couldn't seem to find the words."

Pain clogged her throat. She stared wordlessly at him. Her world spun, and she stumbled as she backed away from him. Grady reached out to steady her, but she flinched at the touch of his hand. For a moment, she thought she saw hurt in his eyes but decided she must have imagined it.

"Stephanie," he tried again, careful to keep his hands to himself even though he longed to take her in his arms. "It isn't how it seems. I know it looks bad, but —"

"Looks bad? Why would you say that, Grady? Just because you came here to spy on me? What were you supposed to do — find out if I were after my mother's money?"

There was enough truth in her charges to cause his face to redden. "It wasn't like —"

"So that's it," she murmured. "You were sent here to spy on me, weren't you?" All color drained from her face, and he feared she was going to pass out.

"Please, let me explain."

"Yes, Stephanie. Let him explain," Trevor seconded. "Tell her how you were going to do it, Chapman."

"I can imagine," she said sarcastically, dredging up a last bit of bravado from somewhere deep inside herself. "How would it go? Something like, 'Sorry, I just happen to have been sent here by your uncle to spy on you, maybe dig up enough dirt to keep you from looking for your mother.' When you couldn't find anything, your boss decides to offer money."

He flinched at her bitterness.

They had both forgotten Tyson. Now he stepped forward. "She's quick, isn't she, Grady?" He favored her with an admiring look.

Stephanie felt sick at his words. "Get out," she whispered hoarsely.

"You heard the lady," Grady told Tyson coldly. "Right now, I'd like nothing better than to throw you out. It's your choice. Make it while you still can."

Tyson stared at him. His breathing turned raspy and labored; a muscle twitched in his throat. For a minute, she thought he was having a heart attack. Miraculously, his face cleared.

"I'll be back," he said. "When you've had a chance to think things over. Make no mistake about it, Stephanie. You're not getting Laura's money."

She bit back a retort, knowing she would only play into his hands by allowing anger to overwhelm her. Instead, she turned her back on him.

With the slamming of the door, she slumped down on a chair. Grady knelt beside her. "You've got to believe me. I never wanted to hurt you."

"Believe you?" She looked incredulously at him. "I believed you once. I'll never make that mistake again."

140

Chilled by the very lack of emotion in her voice, Grady hesitated. He couldn't leave her like this, no matter how much she wanted him out of her sight. She looked physically ill. Self-loathing sluiced over him as he realized he was the cause of it.

"Let me help you," he said, and took her arm.

Too shocked to shake away his hand, she allowed him to help her to the vinyl sofa. To her relief, he didn't sit beside her, but instead straddled the room's one chair, positioning it so that he faced her.

She tried to turn away, but his gaze impaled her own, forcing her to meet his eyes. "Please, say what you have to say. Then leave."

"Tyson was telling the truth. Up to a point." He looked at her closely, trying to determine if she were listening. "He sent me to find you. I . . . agreed. I am — I was — a troubleshooter for Tyson Industries."

"Why didn't he leave well enough alone? I wasn't looking for my natural parents."

"Laura wanted to see you. He wanted to make sure the two of you never found each other."

"Does he really believe I'd try to take her money?"

His silence was answer enough.

"As if I'd care . . . All I ever wanted was to know why she gave me away."

"I know that."

"Then why didn't you tell your boss that her precious money was safe?"

"I tried. But Trevor Tyson believes everyone is motivated by money."

"Like he is?"

"Yeah. Like he is."

"That still doesn't tell me why my . . ." She stumbled over the word. ". . . mother wants to see me after all these years."

"Laura's not been well the last couple of years."

"She's not —"

He shook his head quickly. "She's not dying. But she has degenerative arthritis. I think she wanted to have some time with you while she can still get around."

"So Tyson had you find me before Laura could trace me?"

"Something like that. That was before . . ."

"Before what?"

"Before I fell in —"

Her snort of disbelief stopped him before he could complete the sentence. "I reported back to Tyson that I'd found you. He wanted me to find a way to . . ." He struggled to find the words that wouldn't destroy everything they'd shared.

"To get close to me. Right?"

His shoulders slumped as he realized there were no words. "Yeah. See what you were like. Before we told Laura we'd found you."

"He never intended to tell his sister, did he?"

"No. I didn't know that when I started the job." Too late, he realized his mistake.

"The job. That's all I was to you, wasn't I? A job."

"You know better than that."

"So you were supposed to see what you could use to keep me away from my mother?"

"It wasn't like that."

"No? What *was* it like? You didn't come here to find out about me?"

She saw the truth in his eyes.

"That's how it started."

"And that's how it's ending. Tell me, Grady. What did you report back to your boss? Did you tell him that I spend my days working on old houses and my nights trying to figure out how to meet the pay-roll? Did you tell him that I get my hands dirty and that I like it? Did you —"

"Stop it."

The command took him by surprise as much as it did her. He held out a hand. "It wasn't like that."

"Oh?"

143

"At first, it was only a job. And then —"

"Don't tell me. You fell in love with me."

The scorn in her voice stung but not as much as the pain he saw in her eyes. He deserved whatever she dished out to him. He waited.

"What? Don't you want to deny it?"

"I can't deny falling in love with you," he said in a low voice. "I wanted to tell you, but —" How could he explain being blackmailed without exposing his brother? "There's someone else involved, someone I owe more than I can ever repay. I spun you that yarn about needing a job. I knew you needed a finish carpenter."

At his words, she recoiled as though he had struck her. It *had* all been deliberate. He'd used her. And she'd let him. What a fool she'd been. After years of not letting anyone get close to her, she'd all but invited him into her life.

Something he'd said only now registered. "You knew that Bill Riedman had quit."

A flicker of emotion crossed his face.

Realization came, and with it, a fresh surge of anger. "You arranged it, didn't you? You managed to get Bill away from here and then showed up to take his place."

"It was the only way I knew to get close to you."

"You certainly knew how to worm your way into my life." A tightness in her throat constricted her breathing as she remembered the day he'd appeared at the work site.

At the time she'd thought it was too good to be true — an expert finish carpenter showing up just when she needed one. Now she knew she'd been right. It *had* been too good to be true. Just as Grady had been.

"I wanted to tell you the truth. A hundred times, I wanted to, planned to . . . I even tried to."

"Then why didn't you? You could have told me anytime about Tyson."

"I was afraid. Afraid you'd send me away, afraid of losing my chance with you."

"You got that right," she muttered.

"So you tell me. What was I supposed to do?"

"My heart bleeds for you."

"It's not like you to be so cruel, Stephanie."

"It's not like me to fall in . . ." She swiped angrily at the tears that trickled down her cheeks.

"Love?"

"That's a laugh. I hate you, Grady." Goose bumps raised on her arms as she realized what she'd said. "I've never said that before."

"Right now, I hate myself."

"At least we have something in common."

"I never meant to hurt you."

She hesitated. Maybe, just maybe, he meant what he'd said. Then she hardened her heart against any hint of softening. Even if he did feel real remorse, that didn't change what she was feeling. She'd been lied to, used, and made to feel a fool.

He pulled her to him, his hands clamping her arms to her sides. "You once said you trusted me, that you believed me when I said I loved you. Is this how you show it?"

She gave a mirthless laugh. Summoning all her strength, she pushed against him, but she was no match for him and he held her tight. "You'd do better not to use words like *trust* or *believe* with me. Coming from you, they don't carry much weight."

Her struggles grew more heated as she realized the danger of staying in his arms. She didn't fear he'd hurt her; no, the risk was far greater than that. The longer he held her, the more she remembered the tenderness of his touch, the searing heat of his kisses, the whispered words of love. She couldn't afford the memories.

Fear lent her strength, and she gave one last push. This time, she managed to free herself.

"Good-bye, Grady."

He reached for her, only to stop when she jerked back. "Stephanie, if you'll give me a chance . . ."

He stepped back, taking a hard look at her lifted chin, the challenge that emanated from her eyes. His voice trailed off as he dropped his hand. "It's not over. Not yet."

The lights in the trailer flicked off. After waiting to make sure she was settled for the night, he headed to the work site. Nothing would make up for what he'd done to her, but he could help her meet the deadline on the Patterson place.

He worked steadily, carefully blanking out any thought beyond the job. The dining room wainscoting slowly took shape. A sense of accomplishment filled him even as his heart felt as if it were shattering.

He wished Stephanie were here. She'd understand the feeling of fulfillment that he felt upon seeing the wood come alive under his hands.

When the last nail hole had been filled

and spackled, he stood back to admire his handiwork. It was the best work he'd ever done. Maybe heartache did that for a person, maybe not. He only knew he'd never touch another tool without thinking of Stephanie.

After stowing his toolbox in the back of his pickup, he drove aimlessly, not caring where he went or how he got there. He couldn't stop thinking of the pain reflected in Stephanie's eyes, a pain he'd put there.

Just this morning, she'd told him she loved him. Her eyes had radiated happiness and hope. He remembered the pure joy that had filled him upon hearing those three simple words. He wondered if he'd ever hear them again.

Only a near miss when he allowed his truck to drift too far into the other lane jolted him back to reality.

From then on, he focused on his driving, glad of the concentration required. He made the trip to Los Angeles with only minimal stops for food and rest.

There was one thing he could do for Stephanie and Laura. Under the circumstances, it was the *only* thing he could do.

Stephanie forced herself out of her bed. She'd been a fool. She'd given her heart,

148

her trust, to a man who deserved neither.

She'd walked into it with her eyes open, ignoring Hank's misgivings about Grady and her own better judgment. She had no one to blame but herself. The knowledge didn't lessen her pain.

Never had she felt such pain, not even at the death of her parents. It was a gnawing emptiness that she feared she might never be able to fill.

Ever since the Jamesons had adopted her, her life had been good. Except for her parents and Hank, she'd kept pretty much to herself, leaning on no one, a legacy from her childhood. It had taught her self-reliance at an early age.

In a few short weeks, she'd thrown that all away.

Too intent on helping her dad build up the business and then taking it over when he died, she'd had little time or interest for romantic involvements. Until Grady Chapman had walked into her life.

A shower, as cold as she could make it, and fresh clothes gave her enough energy to head to the work site.

"Hey, Stephanie," Hank called from the porch of the house. "When did you get the wainscoting done?"

She looked at him blankly. "I never got

to it." She'd been too busy trying to put a broken heart back together.

"Well, somebody sure did."

Sure he must be mistaken, she followed him into the dining room. And stared. Not trusting her eyes, she ran her fingers over the meticulously carved wood. Fresh tears sprang to her eyes. *Grady*.

"It was Chapman, wasn't it?" Hank asked. "There's no one else except you who can do this kind of work."

Fortunately, he didn't appear to expect an answer. He ran his hand admiringly over the smooth surface of the wood. "He's one fine craftsman."

"I thought you didn't like Grady," she was surprised into saying.

"I said I didn't trust him. But that doesn't mean I can't appreciate a beautiful piece of work like this. When'd he find time to do it? He must have worked all night."

"He must have," she echoed softly.

"Where is he, anyway? I owe the man an apology. Anyone who'd work overnight to make sure we met the deadline has to be all right."

She swallowed around the wad of emotion in her throat. "He . . . uh . . . had to leave. A family emergency."

150

Hank looked puzzled. "I thought he didn't have any family."

"You thought wrong," she said shortly.

"Sure," he said, giving her a strange look.

"Sorry. I didn't mean to snap at you. I guess I'm a little edgy." She managed a smile. "I didn't sleep much last night."

"Maybe you ought to take a couple of hours off, get rested up. I can pull a couple of men off the Conrad place and finish up here." He gestured to the completed woodwork. "What with that done, we're ahead of schedule." He scratched his head. "Never thought I'd hear myself say that."

"No." Aware that she'd practically shouted the word, she lowered her voice. "I'll feel better once I get to work." The last thing she needed was time to be alone with her thoughts — and her regrets. She'd have a lifetime to spend doing just that.

"Whatever you say."

Aware of his scrutiny, she flushed. "I'll be out in a couple of minutes."

"Sure." He hesitated. "Stephanie?"

"Yes?"

"I'm sorry."

She realized she hadn't fooled him a bit. "So am I."

A week after Grady had left, Stephanie

151

was functioning. Just barely. Thoughts of Grady had infiltrated her dreams as well as her waking hours, turning what sleep she managed to get into pain-filled dreams.

The solution was simple. She simply wouldn't think about him. Of course, ordering herself not to think about him resulted in her being able to think of little else.

She threw herself into her work. Work had always provided a refuge for her in the past. Now, though, it proved as empty as her heart. Still, she kept at it. If she failed to find peace, at least she had the satisfaction of knowing her bank balance had never looked better.

She tightened her belt another notch and decided heartache was more effective than any diet. Putting Grady out of her mind wasn't proving hard. It was proving impossible. But she wasn't a quitter. She'd find a way to live without him. After all, she'd spent the first twenty-eight years of her life without him.

Her musings were cut short as she saw Hank approach. The smile she forced faded abruptly at the scowl she saw on his face.

"You lose much more weight, you'll have to start wearing suspenders to hold your pants up."

She found a smile and pasted it on her lips. "Haven't you heard? Thin is in."

He remained silent.

"Okay, okay," she muttered. "So I've lost a few pounds. It's no big deal."

"It is to those who love you."

The quietly spoken words shamed her. Hank didn't deserve her sarcasm. He was a friend, the best she'd ever had. "I'm sorry."

Awkwardly, he laid a hand on her shoulder. "It's all right."

She resisted the urge to squirm under his assessing look.

"It's Grady, isn't it?"

"I don't want to talk about the creep." It was anger she was feeling, she told herself, but she couldn't keep the pain from her voice.

"Maybe he's not a creep."

"Since when have you started defending him? You never liked him. You said so."

"What I said was that I didn't trust him. He didn't look like a carpenter. Turns out I was right."

"So?"

"So I saw the way he looked at you."

"What way?"

"The same way I look at Cathy, the way a man looks at the woman he loves."

"You're wrong," she said at last. "Grady

doesn't love me. He may have cared about me a little, but love . . ." She shook her head.

"If he doesn't, honey, he gives a darn good imitation of it. A man doesn't look at a woman like that unless he's in love. I ought to know. I've felt that once in my life and look what happened."

She laughed, as she knew he'd intended.

"Now what do you say we go over the new job we're bidding on?"

She flashed him a grateful smile. Hank knew when to change the subject. He'd said what he wanted to. Now he was giving her time to think about it.

They spent the next hour going over costs and estimates. The job was an ambitious one, even more so than the Patterson mansion.

"Looks like we'll be sitting pretty if we get this one," Hank said, gathering up a sheaf of papers after they drafted a tentative bid.

"Real pretty," she agreed. Unable to bear the inactivity of sitting at a desk, she stood and started to pace.

"You all right?"

The innocent words scraped along her nerves. *No!* she wanted to shout. *I'm not all right. I may never be all right again.* But she couldn't say that. Not even to Hank. So she summoned a smile, a pale imitation of the real thing, and said, "Sure." She feigned a yawn. "Guess I'm a little tired."

Hank looked like he wanted to say more but took the hint and left.

Much as she tried to dismiss his words later that evening, she couldn't forget them. The notion that Grady loved her wouldn't vanish. But then neither would the certainty that, despite everything, she loved him.

Chapter Eight

When the call came, she wasn't prepared.

How could she be prepared for a call from a stranger who claimed to be the woman who'd given her life twenty-eight years ago and then given her away?

Stephanie stewed about it for hours before picking up the phone and dialing the number Laura Tyson had left on her answering machine. A few minutes later, she replaced the phone and hoped she hadn't just made the biggest mistake of her life.

No, the biggest mistake had been giving Grady Chapman a job. The flash of pain surprised her. Surely she had started to heal by now. But the pain was there, as swift and sharp as ever. Maybe that was the way with love.

And with that admission, she knew the pain would forever be a part of her. But she would learn to live with it, if for no other reason than she had no choice.

With that acknowledgment, she focused her attention on her upcoming visit.

There was no law that said she had to like the woman, Stephanie reminded herself. She could meet with her, and that would be the end of it. She'd remain detached; after all, Laura had given her away with no more thought than she'd have given to tossing out the garbage.

No, that wasn't fair, Stephanie chastised herself. She didn't know why Laura had given her up. She owed it to the woman to find out. What's more, she owed it to herself.

The flight to California wasn't nearly long enough. Neither was the cab ride to the address scribbled on the much-folded paper clutched in her hand.

The three-story house, its brick mellow with age, was set back from the street, flanked by rose gardens. Palm trees lined the drive. After paying the driver, she walked up a flagstone sidewalk and, after a moment's hesitation, rang the bell.

Stephanie had thought about this moment for most of her life. Now that it was here, she was afraid.

No, that wasn't right. She was terrified.

A capable-looking woman led her into a small sitting room and then discreetly disappeared.

Stephanie took her time looking about the room, noting the petit-point chairs, the fresh flowers, the softly faded Persian rug. All bespoke a quiet taste and elegance.

Much like the woman who sat on a Queen Anne-style sofa.

Laura Tyson was small and delicately built. She was also crippled with arthritis. Even her carefully applied makeup couldn't disguise the lines of pain etched on her face.

Stephanie watched as Laura pushed herself up from the sofa and moved unsteadily toward her, her hands gripping a cane. Stephanie wanted to cross the room and save the older woman the trip that was obviously costing her, but she sensed it was important to Laura to make the journey — however painful.

Stephanie looked at this woman who'd given her life. Her resolve to remain detached vanished under the love — and hint of fear — she saw in Laura Tyson's eyes.

The irony of the situation wasn't lost on her. One moment a woman has a baby and the next she gives up that same baby. Now that woman and her grown child were meeting for the first time.

"Stephanie."

The voice cracked just a little, and Stephanie swallowed the sob that caught in her throat. Laura placed a thin hand on her arm and gestured to the sofa.

Slowly, they made their way back to the sofa, Stephanie's arm wrapped protectively around Laura's waist.

Once seated, Laura leaned back and looked at her daughter. Tears filled her eyes. She dabbed at them with a lace-edged handkerchief.

"I hope you'll excuse the tears of a foolish, sentimental woman. It's just that I've waited so long . . ."

Stephanie felt tears spring to her eyes and blinked them back. "So have I."

"Then we have a beginning."

A beginning. Something to build on. She exhaled sharply.

"You too?" Laura asked. At Stephanie's blank look, she added, "Butterflies."

"A whole flock. Only they're storks."

Their mingled laughter forged a bond, and Stephanie knew it was going to be all right.

"You're beautiful. Even more beautiful than I imagined."

Stephanie smoothed back her unruly curls and wrinkled her nose. "Dad — Ron Jameson — used to say I was cute."

"Fathers always think their little girls are cute," Laura said. "But now you're a beautiful young lady."

"Maybe I take after you." It was true, Stephanie decided. Her mother's features were an older, faded version of her own.

Laura touched her own hair, the soft brown streaked with gray.

"Now you're being kind an old woman."

Stephanie shook her head. "You're not old."

Laura placed a hand on her heart. "In here, I'm old. I've felt old ever since I gave you away."

Stephanie heard the grief in Laura's voice and longed to ease it. "You did what you thought was best."

"No. I did what my brother thought best. I wanted to keep you. You'll never know . . . I was young, barely eighteen, when I met your father. He was older, more experienced. He literally swept me off my feet. A few months later, I found myself pregnant and alone."

"He left you?"

"Without a backward glance."

The words were spoken without rancor, only a quiet acceptance.

"Our parents were already dead. Trevor sent me away to an aunt who lived in San Francisco. I stayed there until you were born." Laura's eyes grew soft and dreamy.

"You had a wisp of hair and the biggest eyes I'd ever seen. I fell in love with you as soon as I held you. I'll always regret that I let Trevor convince me to give you up."

Her words eased a long-buried pain in Stephanie's heart. Her mother had wanted her. How many nights had she lain awake, wondering why her own mother had given her away? Now she knew. She couldn't find it in her to blame Laura. She'd been scared and faced with a decision no young woman should be forced to make.

"I'm not blaming Trevor," Laura said. "It was my fault. I never could stand up to him. He was always strong, forceful, even when he was a boy." She twisted her hands in her lap. "He told me the baby . . . you. . . . would be better off with a mother *and* a father. I believed him." She raised her head to smile tremulously at Stephanie. "You were happy, weren't you, with the Jamesons?"

Stephanie looked at this woman who'd loved unwisely. Another bond between them. Laura had suffered. It was there in her eyes, pain-filled and pleading, in the hesitancy of her voice, in the trembling of her hands.

There wasn't any need to tell her about the long, lonely years in foster homes, the

161

adoption that hadn't worked out. "Yes, I was happy. They were good to me."

"I'm glad. I wondered . . . I'd lay in bed at night and think about you, praying you were happy."

"I was," Stephanie said softly. She couldn't feel any bitterness toward Laura. Once maybe, but not now. "The past is over. We have a future to think about."

"That's right. A future." Laura's eyes glowed with the radiance of happiness. "There's so much I want to tell you, to ask you." Tentatively, she reached for Stephanie's hand. "If you'd like, maybe we can spend some time together before you have to go back to Colorado."

"I'd like that," Stephanie said, a catch in her voice. "I'd like that very much."

With a tensing of her shoulders, Laura shifted positions.

Stephanie winced inwardly at the suffering she read in Laura's eyes. She manufactured a yawn. "If you don't mind, I'd like to lie down for a bit. The trip . . ."

"Of course. We can talk more at dinner." Laura reached for her cane.

Before she could rise, Stephanie was at her side, her hand gently cupping Laura's elbow. She'd done it without stopping to think. Now she wondered if she'd rushed in where she wasn't welcome.

Laura's grateful smile banished any doubts.

It was a step, a small one, but a step all the same to bridge the gulf of twenty-eight years.

A few moments later, she found herself shown to a beautifully appointed bedroom. A finely crocheted spread covered the bed. An adjoining bathroom featured every luxury she could ask for.

But none of her opulent surroundings mattered as Stephanie hugged to her the knowledge that Laura loved her, that she hadn't given her up willingly. With that understanding, years of self-doubt and pain washed away.

They spent a quiet evening, talking, filling each other in on their lives. When the last of the dishes had been cleared away, Stephanie felt Laura's agitation. The time for hard talk had come. In a way she was relieved. Better to get it out of the way before it could cast a cloud over her visit.

Laura led the way to her sitting room. When they'd made themselves comfortable and sipped at their coffee, Laura began. "I know what Trevor did . . . what he tried to do. I don't know what to say, except that I'm sorry. And so ashamed."

163

"You didn't do anything —"

"That's just it. I didn't do anything. I turned to my big brother, just like I've done all my life. I let him take over and because of that, I almost lost you again."

"It wasn't your fault. You didn't know."

"But I should have. When I first raised the question of trying to find you, I should have known Trevor wouldn't go along with it. But I wanted to believe he'd changed. I wanted it so much that I let myself believe him when he said he'd help me find you."

"It's all right," Stephanie said, pressing Laura's hand.

"I've been a fool, but no more. You're here and I'm not letting you go."

She shifted uncomfortably. "Laura, I —"

"That didn't come out right," Laura said quickly. "I sound like a fool, trying to hold on to the daughter I never had. I only meant I'd like us to keep in touch . . . if that's all right with you?"

"More than all right," Stephanie whispered.

"Trevor can't hurt us again. I think he knows that. Now that we've got that out of the way, let's talk about you and Grady Chapman."

"What do you mean?"

"He came to see me two weeks ago, told

me what he'd done. He could have blamed Trevor, but he didn't. Said he accepted full responsibility for everything." She paused as Stephanie digested that. "It didn't take much reading between the lines to know the man's in love with you." Laura studied her daughter's face. "You're in love with him too, aren't you?"

The matter-of-fact way Laura said the words convinced Stephanie she'd be wasting her time denying them. "I was. Don't worry. It's over now."

"Is it?" Laura gave her a shrewd look. "How does Grady feel about that?"

"I doubt he feels anything about it at all."

Laura only smiled. "Except for being in love with you."

"I thought he was. I was wrong."

"Were you?"

"Very wrong," Stephanie added in a low voice.

"I'm new at this mother business, but I've been around long enough to know that you don't stop loving someone just because he's disappointed you."

"He did more than disappoint me. He betrayed me . . . us."

"I can see why you'd feel hurt, but betrayed?" Laura shook her head. "If Grady made a mistake, it was in judgment. He had a decision to make, and he did what he thought was right."

"Was it right to lie to me, to make me fall . . . to make me care for him?" Stephanie flushed at the anger in her voice, but, to her surprise, Laura didn't appear upset.

"Did Grady say why he agreed to —"

"Spy on me?" Stephanie frowned as she tried to recall his words. "He said something about repaying an old debt."

Laura nodded, as if she'd just confirmed something important. "That sounds like Grady." She looked thoughtful.

Stephanie couldn't understand Laura's defense of the man who had schemed to keep them apart. When she said as much, Laura shook her head. "What did Grady say when you asked him why he stayed?"

"He said if he left, Tyson would only send someone else."

"He was right. My brother is nothing if not persistent. He'd have sent someone far more ruthless than Grady."

"Why didn't Grady tell me the truth when we started . . . when we found that we . . ."

"Cared for each other?"

A small nod was all Stephanie was able to manage.

"Maybe he was afraid you'd send him away."

She thought about it. Laura was right. She would have sent him away as soon as he'd told her the truth. And why shouldn't she? He'd used her, lied to her, and then had the gall to ask her to forgive him.

"Have you forgiven me for giving you up?" Laura asked.

Stephanie sensed Laura didn't want an easy answer. "I don't know. I think so."

"Have you wondered then why you're so sure you can't forgive Grady? My betrayal was far worse than his. I gave away my own child out of weakness. Whatever Grady did, he did out of loyalty. Can't you find it in your heart to forgive him?"

Forgive Grady? Laura made it sound so easy. Well, it would be a cold day in . . . The thought went unfinished as Laura laid a frail hand on her arm.

"If you give him the benefit of the doubt, I think you'll see that he'd never betray you. It was Trevor's surprise arrival that complicated things. Otherwise, they might have turned out quite differently."

"Why couldn't he just have told me?"

"If Trevor hadn't shown up when he did, I feel sure Grady would have told you in his own time."

"How can you be so sure?"

"He isn't an easy man, but he has a code of honor that's pretty rare these days."

Unwillingly, Stephanie remembered Grady's promise that they'd finish the Patterson job on time. He'd kept that, even though it meant working long hours every evening, hours she hadn't been able to pay him for.

After she'd ordered him out of her life, he'd stayed and worked through the night to finish the wainscoting in the dining room. Even Hank had been impressed by Grady's drive.

"You're too old for me to try to tell you what to do," Laura said, a wry smile edging her lips. "But maybe you'll take some advice from a friend?" At Stephanie's faint smile, she continued, "Pride makes a cold friend. So does loneliness." She paused. "I ought to know."

"Laura —"

"Promise me you'll think about it, okay?"

Stephanie wanted to refuse, but the appeal in Laura's eyes changed her mind. "I promise."

"Good." Laura rose to her feet, accepting Stephanie's quickly offered help.

"Tomorrow, maybe you'll indulge me in

a dream I've had for a long time?"

"If I can." She waited for the request, but Laura only smiled.

"Tomorrow's soon enough."

The following day, Stephanie found herself trying on a dress in an exclusive boutique. The dress whispered softly against her skin as she slipped it on. She smoothed the peach silk over her hips and twirled around in front of a mirror. "It's beautiful."

"*You're* beautiful," Laura said, her voice husky. "We'll take it," she said to the saleslady.

Stephanie found the price tag discreetly tucked inside the sleeve and gasped. "It's way too much," she whispered.

Laura didn't bother looking at the tag. "It's perfect on you. Please, give me the pleasure of getting it for you."

Stephanie wavered. Laura's voice held such happiness underscored by a hint of pleading that she couldn't refuse. "Thank you. It's the most beautiful thing I've ever owned."

Laura kissed her cheek. "No, thank *you*." She handed the clerk a credit card, then insisted upon buying the accessories needed to complete the outfit.

Stephanie could only watch in

bemusement as Laura selected lingerie and shoes in the same pale peach as the dress. To these she added a fine gold chain.

When Stephanie started to protest this extravagance, Laura turned a beseeching smile on her. "Please. Let me do this. And I have one other favor to ask. I want to treat you to a dinner date tonight with this great guy I know. You'll look gorgeous in this new outfit."

"A blind date?" Laura asked uncertainly. "I don't think —"

"Just one dinner," Laura pleaded. "It's all arranged, and I really want you to meet him."

Stephanie shrugged. "Well, I guess one dinner couldn't hurt. Do you always get your own way?" she teased as their purchases were wrapped.

A faint shadow crossed Laura's face. "Not always."

Instant regret filled Stephanie at her thoughtless question, and she reached for Laura's hand. "I'm sorry."

"Don't be. I have so much to be grateful for. And having you here is the most wonderful gift in the world."

Stephanie wondered what the future held for herself and Laura. The only thing she knew for sure was that she very much wanted a future.

What about a future with Grady? a small voice asked. Did she want one with him as well? She pushed the question to the back of her mind, to be dealt with at a later time.

Still flushed with the excitement of their shopping trip, she and Laura stopped at a tearoom. Reluctantly, Stephanie declined seconds on the scones with clotted cream.

"If I'm going out tonight, I can't have any more," Stephanie said when Laura urged her to have yet another.

Learning that Laura had arranged a date for her with Tim Robbins, a son of one of her friends, had given Stephanie an uneasy feeling. The last thing she was interested in was having dinner with a strange man, no matter how attractive Laura insisted he was.

Her heart was still too bruised, her feelings too uncertain, to allow room for another man in her life. Seeing how important it was to Laura, though, she'd given in.

In the end, Stephanie agreed to another scone. They lingered over their tea for a while longer.

Laura glanced at her watch. "We've got to hurry if you're going to make your date."

Stephanie grimaced. "I'd rather spend the evening with you."

"And pass up dinner with one of the city's most eligible bachelors?" Laura's eyes glimmered with amusement. And something more. A speculative look that had Stephanie frowning.

"I'm not interested in men right now. Eligible bachelors or not."

"Have you wondered why not?"

Laura didn't give her a chance to answer as she started discussing their plans for tomorrow.

An hour later, Stephanie descended the curving staircase of Laura's three-story home, feeling slightly self-conscious in her new finery.

The look in Laura's eyes erased any doubts about her appearance.

"Laura, are you sure you don't mind being alone tonight?" Stephanie asked as they waited for her date.

Laura nodded emphatically. "I've been alone for most of my life. Besides, Tim would never forgive me if you stood him up. You'll knock his socks off."

Stephanie didn't want to knock anyone's socks off.

Laura smiled mistily. "You look beautiful."

That night set the pattern for the next week.

Despite Stephanie's protests that she wanted to spend the time with Laura, she'd gone out nearly every evening with a different date, all arranged by Laura and all at Laura's insistence. Laura seemed to have an endless supply of friends with eligible sons, all of whom claimed to be eager to meet Stephanie.

On her last night there, when she'd held firm to her desire to spend the evening with Laura, Stephanie twisted the gold chain, which she hadn't removed since putting it on. "Can I ask you something?" Without waiting for an answer, she plunged on. "I thought you wanted me to think about . . . about how I feel about Grady."

"I do."

The satisfied tone in Laura's voice confirmed Stephanie's suspicions. "All these dates . . . you set them up just so I'd compare Grady to other men."

Laura gave her a mischievous smile. "What do you think?"

"That you're pretty sneaky."

"I've had a good teacher." The smile in Laura's eyes dissolved at the reference to her brother.

Stephanie bit her lip. The last thing she wanted to do was remind Laura of Trevor Tyson. Upon learning that Stephanie was staying with his sister, Tyson had stormed into the house and demanded she leave. Laura had stood up to him with a quiet dignity that filled Stephanie with pride.

"No more," Laura had said after the scene with her brother. "Trevor's bullied me for the last time."

After that, there'd been no more contact from him.

"So, have any of these gorgeous hunks I've set you up with stolen your heart?" Laura asked, only a trace of sadness lingering in her eyes.

Her smile wry, Stephanie pulled her lacy shawl around her shoulders when the doorbell chimed. "I think you know the answer to that."

Laura reached up to kiss her daughter's cheek. "I think you do too. Don't throw away a chance at love. It doesn't come around that often."

She was glad to be home. Her trailer looked small and dingy compared to Laura's spacious house, but it was home. She pulled a soda can from the refrigerator and rolled it over her forehead. The sun had gone down, but dusk had brought no relief from the heat.

The days she'd spent with Laura had been bittersweet. She thought of the years they'd missed, the years they still had before them. She would always think of Sarah Jameson as her mother, but Laura Tyson had given her life.

One thing was certain. She didn't intend to waste time with regrets. They'd been given a second chance. Laura had taught her something already: a chance at happiness was too precious to waste.

Like she'd done with Grady?

She shoved the idea to the back of her mind, not yet willing to examine what she felt for Grady.

She pored over blueprints with Hank the following day. A yawn escaped before she could clamp her hand over her mouth. She felt Hank's concern and summoned a smile.

"Still not sleeping well?" he asked.

"Well enough." Her answer dismissed the subject. Or it would have, she reflected, if Hank had let it drop.

"It's Grady."

She didn't bother denying it. Not to Hank, who was as close to a big brother as she'd ever have.

"Why don't you knock off early? We're pretty much done here. I can finish up whatever's left."

She looked out the window. The perfect summer day beckoned to her. "You've got yourself a deal."

He seemed about to say something but only squeezed her shoulder. Grateful for his understanding, she gave him a quick smile and headed out to the grove of aspen bordering the property.

The sun's warmth lulled her into settling back against a tree. Her legs stretched out in front of her, she folded her arms behind her head. A soft breeze tickled her cheek. She'd rest here for a moment only . . . just enough to give her energy to go back to work.

She knew Hank was worried about her. It wasn't like her to take off early, even with his encouragement, but then nothing she did — or felt — lately was normal. Her lack of energy was only one of many strange symptoms. She wanted to blame it on the heat, with the temperature nearing a hundred degrees before the sun reached its noonday high. But she knew better.

Grady.

It had been three weeks, four days, and — she checked her watch — three hours since he'd walked out. She consoled her-self that at least she wasn't keeping track of the minutes. The thought caused a stran-gled sob to catch in her throat.

Okay, so she wasn't handling it well. But she would. She was a survivor. She'd spent the first eleven years of her life being shuf-fled between foster homes. It didn't make for security, but it had given her a resil-ience most people never developed.

She'd need every ounce of that now if she was going to put Grady out of her mind. She didn't try fooling herself that she could put him out of her heart as easily. Her heart was proving stubbornly insistent in recalling every detail about him. Like the way his hair fell across his forehead when he'd threaded his fingers through it. Like the way a smile spread slowly over his lips before reaching his eyes. Like the way —

"Hey, boss. Thought I might find you here."

The sound of Hank's voice roused her from her thoughts. She pushed herself up, brushed the grass from her jeans, and forced a smile on her face. "What's up?"

"A new job." The grin on Hank's lips nearly split his face in half. "Got the call just now. I took down the particulars, but the guy wants you to give him a call." He grabbed her around the waist and swung her around. "We're rolling."

"You bet we are." She shook off her melancholy. She had a future to look to. If it didn't include Grady, well, she'd learn to live with that.

"Sally Patterson said you're the best there is," Harvey Jackson said when she met with him the following day. "Do what you have to do to get the old place in shape."

The job, renovating a mansion located in downtown Colorado Springs, was a dream come true. Unlimited funds and instructions to "spend whatever it takes" promised to make it a pleasure to restore the mansion to its former glory.

"Thank you," she said, unable to believe her good fortune. A job like this meant making a big chunk in the outstanding loan and maybe even buying some new equipment.

When she told the rest of the crew the extent of the job, they whooped with excitement. "This means a raise for everyone," she said. "Not a huge one, but big enough." She turned to Hank. "I know this isn't enough to keep you here forever, but maybe —"

"It's plenty," he said. "You don't know how much I was hoping for something like this. Leaving you and Legacies was gonna be the hardest thing I'd ever had to do."

A little of the burden weighing on her heart eased. "Thanks."

The Jackson restoration required every bit of skill and vision she possessed. She spent hours in the library, poring over architectural digests dating back to the last century. In a genealogical book on the Jackson family, she found what she was looking for — a detailed account of the original plans for the Jackson mansion.

Armed with illustrations and descriptions of houses of that era, she began sketching. When she was satisfied, she took out her drafting tools and plotted the drawings. Someday she hoped to get a computer-aided drafting program and plotter. Until then, she'd continue to do it the old-fashioned way.

Two years at trade school had given her the skills to feel comfortable with drafting, though it would never be her favorite part of the design process. It was the sight of the wood, the feel of it, the smell of it, that would always provide the inspiration for her.

She had so many dreams, plans, and

hopes. With the successes of the last few months, she dared believed she could make them happen. She only wished she had someone with whom she could share the satisfaction of seeing her dreams come true.

Chapter Nine

Grady loosened his tie. He'd kept tabs on Stephanie through Laura. He wasn't proud of it, but he had to know how Stephanie was feeling, what she was doing.

The idea to meet for lunch had been his. When he'd phoned Laura, she hadn't seemed surprised. In fact, she'd sounded like she'd been expecting his call. She'd chosen a quiet place, a far cry from the usual upscale restaurants favored by her brother.

She was waiting for him when a hostess showed him to the table.

"You look like you've been run over by a truck," Laura said without preamble.

He smiled wryly. "Thanks. I won't return the sentiment. You look wonderful." It was true, he reflected. Her eyes sparked with life. The shadow of pain was still there, but it was now overshadowed by happiness.

"I *feel* wonderful," Laura said. "And it's all because of you. You brought my daughter back to me." At the concern in his eyes, she gave a quick shake of her head. "Don't worry. I don't intend to play mother at this late date. It's enough that we've found each other, that someday we might be friends." She pressed his hand. "Thank you, Grady. You'll never know . . ."

He shifted uncomfortably as tears glistened in her eyes. "I didn't do anything, Laura. Stephanie came to see you because she wanted to."

"You found her." Laura's voice turned husky. "I'll never be able to thank you enough."

He was grateful when the arrival of the waitress forestalled any further expressions of gratitude. They gave their orders and made small talk.

When the food arrived, Grady made a pretense of eating until the question uppermost in his mind would no longer be denied. "How is she?"

The smile that parted Laura's lips wasn't what he expected. But then, nothing that had happened since he'd accepted the job to find Stephanie had been what he'd expected.

"Why don't you ask her for yourself?"

"You know why," he said in a low voice. "She hates me."

Laura's smile widened. "I've always thought you were a pretty smart guy, Grady. Looks like I was wrong."

"Okay. So maybe she doesn't hate me. But I sure don't head her list of favorite people."

"How do you know? Have you asked her?"

Hope flared in his chest, only to die again as he remembered the bitterness in Stephanie's voice when she'd ordered him out of her life. "What're you saying?"

"Love sometimes makes us say things we don't mean."

Love.

At one time he'd believed it had no place in his life. Then he'd met Stephanie. Her love had reached out to wrap itself around him. And he'd allowed himself to hope.

He wanted to hate Laura for causing that hope to spring to life again when he knew it had no chance of fulfillment. But the genuine caring he saw in her eyes wouldn't permit it.

"I'm glad you're happy," he said, meaning it. "You deserve it."

"So do you. I told Stephanie something, but I don't think she heard me. She was hurting. Reach out and embrace life with both hands. If you don't . . ." Her shrug was eloquent.

She didn't finish. She didn't need to.

With the arrival of their food, they

turned the conversation to other topics. Though he longed to hear more about Stephanie, he wasn't sorry to drop the subject of his feelings for her. Laura saw far too much, and right now his defenses were at an all-time low.

He was still mulling over what Laura had told him when her voice interrupted his thoughts.

"I've watched you for a long time, Grady. You don't give of yourself easily. You're a loner."

He nodded shortly.

Working things out on his own was so ingrained that he'd rarely questioned it. He'd always figured it was the right thing to do. Now he wasn't so sure.

"You're used to going your own way, explaining to no one, even when it would clear things up between you and the woman you love."

"I don't —"

The look she gave him put a halt to the rest of the lie.

"Stephanie needs you. What's more, she loves you. Don't you think it's time you started telling her the truth? Like what my brother had on you to make you agree to spy on her."

"You know about that?"

"I know you'd never agree to something like that unless he had a powerful hold on you."

There was more to Laura Tyson than he'd reckoned with.

"Tell me," she ordered softly.

Strangely, he found himself doing just that.

"So he threatened to tell the authorities about your brother. How long are you going to keep paying for a mistake a green boy made twenty years ago?"

It was the same question he'd asked himself over and over during the last weeks.

"Trevor's my brother, but I'm not blind to his faults. I let him talk me into giving away my child, and I've regretted it every day since. Don't make the same mistake." She waved her hands impatiently at his protest. "You know what I mean. If you love Stephanie, tell her."

"Don't you think I tried?"

The words were wrenched from him, and only then did he realize he'd shouted them. Other diners turned to stare at him, and he flushed.

Laura didn't appear embarrassed, though. He could have sworn he saw a hint of a smile chase across her lips before she said, "Then it's up to you to make her believe you. Or won't your pride let you?"

He winced at the truth in her rebuke. The lady didn't pull her punches. Apparently, she had some of the colonel in her after all.

When Stephanie had refused to listen to him, he'd let her get away with it, disappearing from her life like a whipped dog with his tail between his legs.

"The truth hurts, doesn't it?"

"Yeah." He managed a smile. "Yeah, it does."

"I'm sorry. Hurting you is the last thing I wanted to do, especially when you . . ." She dabbed at her eyes with her napkin.

"Laura, you don't have to —"

"Please, let me finish. You've given me back my life." She leaned across the table to brush a kiss on his cheek. "Whatever happens between you and Stephanie, remember that I'll always be grateful for what you did."

After seeing Laura home, Grady mentally replayed his conversation with her. What if she were right about Stephanie's feelings for him?

He owed it to her — and to himself — to find out.

The VA hospital, set in the lush hills of

California's wine country, was better than most. For that, Grady was grateful. He had a spread not far from there where David spent the months when he wasn't being pricked and poked.

The visit to see his brother wasn't something he'd planned. But after talking with Laura, he knew he needed to find a way to set to rest the ghosts of the past.

He found David in the hospital solarium where he was scowling at a computer screen.

When he saw Grady, he flicked the machine off. "I've been wondering when you'd show up. Didn't expect you to come here, though."

Grady flushed. He deserved that. He didn't like seeing his brother in the hospital and usually reserved his visits for the times David was at the ranch.

"Anything wrong with a guy wanting to see his big brother?"

"Nothing wrong at all."

Grady backed away from the reason for his visit and talked about other things, all the while sensing David's impatience, until his brother held up a hand.

"You've done the small talk bit, so why don't you tell me why you're really here?"

Grady looked at the brother he'd idolized, then pitied, and finally accepted as simply a man with human frailties, and that was when the realization hit him. David didn't need his protection any longer.

Lines of pain grooved his face, mute evidence of the years of operations and therapy. With the pain, though, came strength. It was that which Grady had been blind to. Perhaps he'd needed to be needed. Whatever his reasons, it was plain David didn't need — or want — someone to shield him from life any longer.

David uttered something crude after Grady told him of Tyson's blackmail. "You see these?" He pulled back the blanket covering his lap and pointed to the stumps of his legs.

For his brother's sake, Grady had learned years ago not to flinch at the sight.

"Yeah."

"I lost them because I was running away. Not because of some act of bravery, like the medal says. And it's time I started owning up to it. Little brother, you need someone to kick you in the rear." David laughed, a rich, full sound that had Grady joining in. "I'd do it, but I haven't got the equipment. You've got a blind spot about me." He spaced the words out. "You got that? It wasn't your fault. It was mine. Only mine."

Grady balled a fist into his open palm. "You lost your legs, almost lost your life. You didn't deserve what Tyson could do to you."

"Who should pay for my cowardice? It happened. And I'm not so bad off. A lot of guys came home in body bags." David slapped the arm of his wheelchair. "Now let's talk about what you *are* guilty of."

Wary, Grady raised his head.

"It's been twenty years and you still treat me like the invalid you think I am."

He wanted to deny it but recognized the truth in the charge. "What do you want me to do?"

"Cut it out." The vehemence in David's voice shook Grady. More mildly, David added, "I love you for it. But it's time I started standing on my own two legs." He glanced down. "Figuratively, of course."

The dry note in his voice drew a reluctant laugh from Grady.

"I'll let you in on a secret. I've been writing a book. Got a nibble from a couple of publishers. In another year or so, your big brother's gonna be rolling in dough."

Grady clapped him on the back. "Congratulations."

"Now that we've straightened me out, let's talk about you." David subjected Grady to an intense scrutiny, a slow smile spreading across his freckled face. "You met someone."

David's blunt statement startled Grady into asking, "How'd you know?" He'd meant to ease into revealing that he'd met the woman he intended to marry. Instead, David had stolen his thunder with the three words.

His brother snorted in exasperation. "I can't walk. That doesn't mean I'm blind. Get real, man. It's right there on your face."

David's legs might be gone, but everything else was working just fine, Grady thought.

"So give. What's she like?"

"She's beautiful, smart, talented —"

"Do you love her?"

"Yes."

"Does she love you?"

That one was tougher to answer. "She did. I'm not so sure anymore."

"You screwed up," David guessed.

"Yeah. Big time."

"Want to talk about it?"

"Yeah. I do."

The story came out in bits and pieces.

Grady didn't spare himself in the telling.

A tuck furrowed itself between David's brows. "You agreed to spy on the woman and ended up falling in love with her?"

"That's about it."

"And now she hates your guts."

"I don't know. I thought she did. I'm hoping I'm wrong."

"So go see her, convince her she's the only woman for you, and ask her to forgive you." David slapped his brother's arm. "Now get out of here so I can get back to work. You've got a lady to see. And I've got some calls to make."

"Do you want me —"

The look in David's eyes was enough to stop Grady's offer of help. "Whatever happens, I can deal with it."

After hugging his brother, Grady turned to go.

"Hey, Grady?"

"Yeah?"

"When you square things with your lady, don't forget to invite me to the wedding."

"You got it."

She was feeling stronger, Stephanie reflected. She rarely thought of Grady anymore. Her lips quirked in a self-derisive smile. No more than twenty or thirty times an hour, at any rate.

Of course she had moments of missing him, but they were getting fewer. Definitely fewer. Yes, she congratulated herself, she was handling it well. In another week . . . two at the most . . . she'd hardly spare a thought for him.

The expectation shouldn't have left her feeling so unhappy. She wasn't exactly depressed, she reminded herself, just at loose ends. The Jackson job was coming along nicely. Mr. Jackson had even promised a bonus if they finished the job ahead of schedule. She should have been celebrating.

But some days, like today, when the sun blossomed through the clouds with such determination, when the air was heavy with the scent of roses and fresh earth, when the birds sang so sweetly, it was difficult to forget Grady. He had come into her life just as the weather had hinted of spring. And he had left when the season was ripening to its fullness.

If she felt tears prick her eyes occasionally, well, it was hay fever season. She certainly didn't need to apologize for having an allergy. Funny, she'd never been bothered by hay fever before, but there was a first time for everything.

A first time for falling in love.

She squashed the thought as soon as it formed, but she was too late. Memories of Grady assailed her. She let them have their way. Maybe if she unleashed them, they'd lose their power over her . . . and maybe the moon really was made of green cheese.

The memories tumbled together, one on top of the other. The two of them framing rooms together. Sharing a sandwich on a lunch break. Sneaking away to spend a few moments alone together free from the pressures of the job. She examined each mind-picture with painful thoroughness.

Why couldn't she let them go?

Okay, you love the guy. Admit it and get it over with. That done, she decided she felt better. Now if only she could convince her heart of it. But it was proving more stubborn than she anticipated. It clung to the fantasy she'd conjured up of Grady and she as a couple, making a family together.

In the weeks since she'd visited Laura, she'd frequently wondered if she'd judged him too harshly. Maybe she should have given him a chance to explain. It was too late now. Even if she wanted to contact him, she had no idea where he was.

Impatient with her melancholy, she stood and brushed the grass from her jeans. What she needed was to get back to work. There were specs for the Jackson place she wanted to go over one more time. There was the ad to check before she placed it in the newspaper.

A strangled laugh caught in her throat as she thought of the job advertisement she'd put together that morning — an ad for a finish carpenter. She should have placed it weeks ago. Oh, she'd had reasons why she couldn't do it then, when Grady had walked out on the job. And out on her. The truth was she couldn't bring herself to write the words that signaled the end of what they'd shared.

It was time to get on with life, she chastised herself. Grady was gone. The sooner she dealt with that, the better off she'd be. With that pep talk firmly in mind, she started back to the job site.

A movement in the woods bordering her house caught her attention. She stopped, staring as the figure took shape.

For a moment, she thought she was imagining it. He was there. Standing in the grove of trees flanking the house, his hair glinting in the sunlight, he looked so good that it was all she could do not to throw herself in his arms. Who was she fooling with all that talk about being over him?

She wanted him — loved him — as much as she ever had. Seeing him now, she knew she always would.

Maybe it was time she started listening with her heart, she thought, remembering Laura's words. Maybe it was time she started listening *to* her heart.

She started walking. Slowly at first. Her pulse quickened as her pace picked up. Then she was running. His arms opened. She didn't stop, didn't question, didn't think.

And then she was there. In his arms. His mouth on hers. She knew it didn't matter how he'd come into her life. Or why. All that mattered was that he was there. All that mattered was that they loved each other.

Love didn't question; love accepted. And that was what she intended to do.

How long they stayed there, locked together, she didn't know. Didn't care. Minutes, hours — they were all the same.

"Grady —"

"Stephanie —"

She looked at him with sudden shyness. "You first," she said.

"No, you."

"I'm sorry." As soon as she said the words, she felt as if a weight had been lifted from her heart.

"I'm the one who's sorry."

She silenced his apology with a quick kiss. "It doesn't matter anymore. You're here."

"For as long as you'll have me."

"How long is forever?"

In answer, he gathered her into his arms again, kissing her with such intensity that she wondered how she'd ever doubted his love.

"You're sure?" he asked when he released her only long enough that he could see her face.

"More sure than I've ever been of anything in my life." She heard the whoosh of relief as he let out a breath. "How about you? Are you sure you want to get tied up with a woman who wears sawdust instead of perfume?"

He made a production of sniffing behind her ear. "I always liked the smell of sawdust."

"I wear jeans seven days a week. When I'm working on a job, I forget what time it is — sometimes, what day it is." She knew she was babbling, but she couldn't seem to stop herself. "I —"

"Talk too much." He kissed her again, a brush of lips that had her wanting more.

"It's time I told you about Tyson."

"You don't have to."

"I owe you an explanation."

"You don't owe me anything."

"I want to. I have to."

She recognized the steel thread of determination running through his voice. She didn't want to hear about the hold Tyson had over Grady. That was the past. But she sensed no amount of talking would convince him otherwise.

"Okay."

He rubbed a hand over his jaw. "Trevor Tyson was my commanding officer in Grenada. When I got out, I bummed around for a while. I tried just about everything, but nothing seemed to click. Then I ran into Tyson in LA and he offered me a job. I've been working for him ever since."

"What you told me about being a troubleshooter —"

"Was the truth. I really am a troubleshooter. For Tyson Industries. I did special jobs for him."

"Special jobs?" Was that what she was?

He shook his head, apparently reading her mind. "You were never a special job. Not in that way. Not from the first time I saw you. But you *were* special."

"I don't understand."

197

"You were different right from the start. When I first saw you, I knew that this was going to be different. I tried to tell myself nothing had changed. That you were an assignment and nothing more."

"But . . ."

"Something happened."

"What?"

"I fell in love with you. I wanted to walk away from the job. From Tyson Industries. From the old man. From everything. But I couldn't leave.

"I told you about David. All the time we were growing up, he was my hero. He could do no wrong, at least in my eyes. He was the one who held us together after my mom died. When he enlisted, it wasn't the popular thing to do. It wasn't fashionable back then to want to serve in the Marines. But he did. I wasn't very old, but I remember the protest marches, the antiwar mania the whole country was caught up in. But he went ahead because he believed in what he was doing.

"I remember the letters he wrote home. He said that nothing was how it was supposed to be. The officers didn't know what they were supposed to be doing half the time. Orders from Washington came and then were revoked. The politicians came, made the correct noises, and then went home without doing anything.

"Despite all the craziness going on, he didn't let it get him down. Not at first anyway. Not until —" The pain that filled his eyes had her reaching for him. "When he came home . . . without his legs . . . I tried to make everything right. But it didn't work. David started taking drugs, got caught up in that whole scene. It got worse until I couldn't take care of him anymore. I ended up putting him in rehab. He hated me for it. For a long time, he refused to even see me."

She waited, knowing there was more to come.

"The last few years, everything's been better. David seemed happier, more at peace with himself. He took some classes and became a computer programmer. I thought that things were finally coming together for him."

Seeing what it was costing him, she laid a hand on his arm. "You don't have to tell me any more."

He squeezed her hand and smiled faintly. "I got a call from Tyson. When I saw him and he told me what he wanted, I refused. Something about it . . . I don't know . . . it didn't feel right. That's when he pulled out a letter. It was from a man in David's platoon in 'Nam. He must have been saving it for years, something to use when I didn't toe the line. I didn't know how he got a hold of it. I didn't much care."

She was scarcely aware of holding her breath. Grady seemed to have slipped into the past, his eyes distant and unfocused.

"It said . . . David was a coward. That he lost his legs when he was running from enemy fire, in the same skirmish that earned him the medal for bravery.

"I couldn't believe it. I told Tyson it was nothing but a pack of lies and what he could do with it."

"Maybe you were right and it wasn't true."

"He pulled out a stack of papers, backing up what the letter said."

"Why didn't the man who wrote the letter do anything about it?"

"He died before he ever had a chance to take it any higher. I kept telling myself that David couldn't have lied all these years about what happened."

"Why didn't you call him?"

"I did. As soon as I told him the name of the guy who'd written the letter, he went real quiet. Then he started to cry." A shudder rippled through him. "Do you know what it's like to hear the brother you love more than life itself cry like a baby?"

"What did you do?"

"I told him I'd take care of it."

"You didn't ask him if it —"

"If it was true? No. I couldn't. I was too afraid. I hung up and told Tyson I'd do the job."

"And then you came here."

"Yeah."

"I wish you'd told me. We could've worked it out together."

"So do I. A thousand times, I wanted to. I've never been blackmailed before. Once you're in, you feel like there's no way out. I kept trying and only dug myself in deeper."

Her hand found his. "It's over. What happens now? With David?"

"I went to see him, told him what Tyson was threatening."

"What'd he say?"

"That it was time to tell the truth. He said he always knew it would come out sometime. He sounded sort of relieved. Like it was something he'd wanted to do for a long time."

Tyson had played on Grady's loyalty to his brother. She should have known that his loyalty would run deep, especially to the brother he idolized. She swiped at her eyes with a balled-up fist, but the tears came anyway. She cried. For David. For Grady. For herself. "It wasn't your fault," she said at last, "what happened to David."

"I've finally figured that out."

"You told me once to let go of the past," she said softly. "It's my turn now. It's time to let it go."

He brought her hand to his lips. "You're right. Maybe now I can. I went through life, doing my job, but never really caring for anyone except David since I got discharged. I thought all that had died a long time ago — at least for me." The warmth in his eyes sent waves of longing through her. "Until I met you."

"What will you do now?"

"I've saved most of my salary over the last ten years." His lips quirked into a tight smile. "Not much to spend it on except a small spread I keep near the hospital. I was thinking of maybe going into business."

"What kind of business? Maybe I could help."

"Maybe you could. What I'd really like to do is to put it into a small business that I have an interest in." He cocked his head to one side. "Do you have any ideas?"

Her lips curved into a smile. "I just might have one or two."

"Good."

"I've been thinking about taking on a partner." She drew her brows together, pretending to consider the matter. "Of course, it'd have to be the right kind of partner. Someone who knows his way around the business. Someone who can oversee a project from beginning to end."

"Did you have anyone in particular in mind?"

"Someone very particular."

"Anyone I know?"

Her eyes shone. "You. And me. To-gether."

"You mean it?"

"More than I've ever meant anything in my life."

His hand closed around hers. "Part-ners."

"Partners."

"A partnership should be sealed."

A tiny frown stitched a furrow between her brows. "You mean a contract —"

"I mean this." The kiss was everything she'd dreamed about during the long weeks they'd been apart.

He wouldn't be an easy man, she thought. Never easy. His pride and honor demanded too much of him for that. But he would love her with passion and energy and would expect the same from her.

"This is a lifetime contract," he warned her. "Permanent and binding."

Everything within her became hushed with joy at the love she saw in his eyes. "You drive a hard bargain," she whispered.

"I'm not bargaining," he said, his strong voice sounding suddenly vulnerable. "I'm begging. Spend the rest of your life with me."

It was no hardship at all to agree.